CTHULHU EXPLAINS IT ALL

The Collected Advice Columns of *Dear Cthulhu*

Vol. 5

PATRICK THOMAS

PADWOLF
PUBLISHING

PADWOLF PUBLISHING INC.
WWW.PADWOLF.COM
www.facebook.com/Padwolf

WWW.PATTHOMAS.NET
WWW.DEARCTHULHU.COM

www.facebook.com/PatrickThomasAuthor

I_PatrickThomas @ Twitter

CTHULHU EXPLAINS IT ALL
The Collected Advice Columns of Dear Cthulhu Vol. 6

© 2019 Patrick Thomas

Portions of this book have appeared in column form in the following magazines: Tales From The Talisman, Nth Degree, and The Realm Beyond.

Book edited by John L. French

Cover Art by Patrick Thomas

Dear Cthulhu is © & TM Patrick Thomas

ISBN 10 digit 1-890096-83-0 and 13 digit 978-1-890096-83-0
First printing. Printed in the USA

If you have any additional questions that Cthulhu can answer, and Cthulhu can answer all questions, Dear Cthulhu welcomes letters and questions at DearCthulhu@ dearcthulhu.com. All letters become the property of Dear Cthulhu and may be used in future columns. Sending financial offerings along with your questions is not necessary but is always appreciated.

Anyone foolish enough to follow Dear Cthulhu's advice does so at their own peril.

Dear Cthulhu,

My kids are five and six years old and their father and I recently divorced. He ran off with our milk woman. Although truth be told I'm not sure if she actually was a milk woman or if that was the story they made up when I came home early one day caught her in our kitchen helping herself to the milk in our refrigerator. I honestly don't think there are any working dairy delivery people anymore.

Anyway, it was a tough time for both me and the kids and they had been wanting a dog. I broke down and got them a puppy. They named him Rags. They loved this dog and he was a mutt with all sorts of unique spots and markings unlike anything I've ever seen before. They didn't want to leave him long enough to go to school so I brought Rags in the car when I dropped them off at school. Then I took him home before I went to work.

One morning after the kids got off okay, I rushed home so I could drop the puppy off and still make it to work on time. Rags was in the front passenger seat with his paws up on the door and his little head hanging out the window. Because he was such a small thing, when I hit a pothole on the highway poor Rags got thrown out the window. Rags was wearing his leash which was hooked on the emergency brake. I thought it was short enough to make sure he stayed in the car, but I misjudged. The poor thing fell out the window and his neck snapped, killing him instantly.

I called in sick to work and tried to find another puppy that looked just like Rags but like I said he was pretty unique and I couldn't do it.

So when I picked the kids up at school, I had to tell them that Rags ran away. I may have bitterly added under my breath that he probably ran off with the milk woman.

I didn't realize the kids heard me until the next visitation with her father when they accused his slut of stealing their dog and told her she had to give Rags back.

It's caused quite the rift with their father and his dairy whore. I don't know if I should come clean and tell the kids he died because we've been going out every day to look for him and have posted lost dog posters on every telephone pole in town. I even offered to get them a new puppy but they said they didn't want to so Rags wouldn't be upset when he came back.

What should I do?

-Mama Dog-mangler in Matilda

Dear Matilda,

You are the parent and that means you are in charge. Tell your offspring that you got a notice from the police that the dog died. You didn't mention what you did with the body but if you can still get a hold of it, give the children closure and bury the pet in the backyard. If you can't, burn something and put in an urn and tell them it is Rags. Dump the ashes in your backyard, have a little service, and move on.

If they still want, get them a new puppy. It sounds like you did not have the first one long so within a month your offspring will be just as happy with it. Although from now on drive with the windows closed and the doors locked when the dog is in the car.

For Dr. Howard Margolin-

Thanks for letting Dear Cthulhu be on the radio

Dear Cthulhu,

I'm a real pickle of a dilemma. I sort of killed my boyfriend but at the time I did it I thought it was self-defense. We were into a lot of role-playing where we'd meet at a bar like we never met each other before then act out a situation, like he's a sailor and I'm a lion tamer. You know the usual stuff.

My cell phone was way old and I was up for a new one which is when they always start to break down, so I wasn't getting my texts right away. Sometimes it took a few hours from when someone sent it to when my phone actually let me know about it.

I'm usually the last one off work at my job at the mall. It was late at night and I was walking to my car when some guy in a hoodie came up and assaulted me. The lunatic told me he was going to take me right there.

I sort of freaked out. The mall parking lot's not in the best shape so I bent down and picked up a broken piece of the asphalt. I swung it as hard as I could and smashed the lunatic in the head. I must have hit him pretty hard because I killed him.

Then when I pulled off the hoodie, I realized it was my boyfriend, Lawrence. I sort of freaked out. That's when my phone buzzed and I got the text he sent me three hours earlier about how he wanted to role-play this very situation.

I know I should've just called the cops and explained what happened but instead, I opened my car door, popped the trunk, and dragged his body into it. Then I shut the trunk.

When I got in the driver's seat to take off, my key wouldn't start the car, which when I realized it wasn't my car, just the same make and color. I had parked three aisles over so I walked casually so as not to draw attention to myself and figured I'd drive over and transfer the body into my trunk.

Unfortunately, in the time that took, the 65-year-old retired woman who owned the first car came out of the mall and drove home. Two days later when she opened up her trunk to put groceries in, she found the body. She called the cops but they charged her with the murder. I thought for sure they'd review the security footage from the mall and it would point to me but it turns out that the camera was vandalized and didn't work. That woman is going to trial and I feel guilty. If I come forward this woman wouldn't have to go to jail but I would. I'm torn between my freedom and doing the right thing. What should I do?

    – Killer Girlfriend in Kokomo

Dear Kokomo,

You have to decide is which is more important to you – a clear conscience or being able to come and go as you please. You might be able to argue self-defense, especially if you can prove the time he sent the text versus the time you received it. However, there would still be the possibility that you would end up in prison.

You would also have to explain why you would put the body in someone else's car and why you didn't call the police. I would advise claiming that you were planning on rushing him to the hospital and then realized it was the wrong car then became so overcome by grief that you were not able to think reasonably. When you were, you realized it was too late to call the police. I would advise spending a lot of money on a very good lawyer. On the plus side for the older woman, she has less time left to spend in jail and at least is guaranteed healthcare there which is sadly not a given in your country.

Dear Cthulhu,

I'm a senior in high school in a small farming community. We only have one traffic light and it's the blinking kind. There is nothing to do here except drink and get stupid. My friends and I have actually gotten very good at this.

One night we were drunk and decided to go out cow tipping. It seemed like a good idea at the time, but it ended in disaster. We snuck into Farmer Tan's fields with the intention of tipping a few cows and getting gone. There was one cow that we saw and we snuck up and started to push her over. Before she could fall, we heard a snorting behind us and realized the reason there was only one cow in the field was because it was in heat and Farmer Tan had left alone her alone with the bull. The bull must have been upset that we were touching his cow friend and came after us. We scattered, but Josh was drunker than the rest of us and ended up running around in circles, trying to find the exit instead of climbing the fence.

The bull took him, tossed him with his horns, and then stomped on top of him. I jumped back inside and distracted the bull, while my other buddies pulled Josh out. We got him in the car and rushed him to the hospital, which was forty-five minutes away. Josh didn't make it. He was gone by the time we got there. We left him in a wheelchair outside the emergency room. We heard a siren, probably an ambulance, and we freaked out and ran away.

It was in the papers that the cops are conducting a murder investigation because they think he was the victim of gang violence because of being gored and beaten so badly by the bull.

I realize we should have stayed and explained what happened, but we didn't. If we do it now we'll probably get in trouble for leaving Josh there. Part of me wants to confess and part of me wants to run away and forget it ever happened. What should I do?

    – Cow Tipping Coward in Canisteo

Dear Tipping,

You will undoubtedly have great difficulty if you simply confess what you have done. Humans are often more lenient on the younger members of your species, but not always. Several factors could be weighed including the mood of the judge and DA and your own personal history – for instance, if you have been in trouble with the law before they are more likely to be harder on you. Another thing that would go in your favor is if your skin was what they would consider the right tone and if your parents or extended family were all wealthy and influential.

Humans in power tend to give breaks to others in their circle. The truth of the matter is, had you not run, a lot of you were guilty of nothing more than stupidity, something which humans are not only proficient in but seem to take great pride in. None of you should have been in the pasture in the first place, but you did rescue Josh from the creature who was attacking him and attempted to save his life.

I suggest you contact an attorney for legal advice and have the lawyer act as an intermediary, perhaps having a deal in place where you avoid prosecution by revealing the facts of the case, which should be able to be backed up eventually by forensic evidence.

One other thing to consider is that your friend's family would have the opportunity to go after the farmer for the death of their son and get money. While there are many of your species who would much rather have an offspring rather than large amounts of cash, the opposite is sometimes true. Although money will not bring back their son, it does seem to lessen the blow with your species. In fact, the rest of you might have a class action suit against the farmer for trauma suffered. In fact, you should perhaps seek treatment for posttraumatic stress syndrome before going to the lawyer. Then you would be able to blame your actions on that and it would help you avoid charges. And once all this is sorted out, if you are looking for gainful employment considering your actions in protecting your friend from the bull, you may want to consider becoming a rodeo clown. You seem to have a knack for it.

Dear Cthulhu,

I'd been dating this girl for six months but she didn't know it. Some people might not consider it dating. They might prefer the term "stalking" but they just don't understand our love.

My girlfriend "Susie" did a lot of volunteer work, especially at the local animal shelter which includes doing community outreach and trying to get people to adopt the different animals. I finally got the courage to introduce myself to her after almost four months into our relationship. It was at a town fair.

Susie said I should adopt a lovely cat named Tabby. She called the cat "lovely". I would have said mildly cute. When Susie handed Tabby to me to hold, she touched her hand to the back of mine. It was like fireworks went off inside my head and the entire world faded. From my point of view, it seemed like Susie was actually bathed in light. The next few minutes were a blur but apparently, I agreed to adopt the cat and even signed paperwork to that effect.

I didn't want to go back and return the cat as I figured that might reduce the risk of Susie eventually marrying me, so I took Tabby home. I have to admit I wasn't exactly thrilled at the prospect of taking care of another being, but I got used to it. More than that.

I'm not good with people so I don't have many friends. Those I do have – like Susie – are not always aware of our friendships. Tabby actually likes me. At night when I watch TV, he crawls in my lap and when I go to sleep at night he lays in the crook of my legs or arms and sleeps next to me. It's wonderful to finally have something that cares about me.

It also gave me the courage to go back and invite Susie to join Tabby and me for dinner. When I got to the shelter I got the worst news of my life. Susie had kept something very important from me. She had another stalker and that jerk killed her. I did feel somewhat guilty about the whole situation. I had neglected our relationship – basically, me stalking Susie from a distance –

to instead take care of Tabby. If I hadn't, maybe I would've seen the other stalker and would have been able to stop him before he killed her.

I guess even worse and more disgusting, the other stalker left the body in her apartment and Susie had five cats of her own. After she was dead for a couple days the cats ran out of food and they ate her face off.

When I went home I looked at Tabby differently. I couldn't help it. I'm worried that if I die, Tabby will eat my face off. The constant worrying is affecting our relationship. I'm concerned that one of the only reasons Tabby likes me is because he's waiting for me to die so he can chew on my cheeks and my forehead.

What should I do?

– Paranoid of a Tabby in Tacoma

Dear Paranoid,

You are worrying about something that is basically a waste of your time. The cat likes you partially for your companionship and partially because you're taking care of his physical needs such as food, water, and providing a litter box. I doubt the cat has enough higher cognitive function to be planning to wait for your demise to eat part of you. The cats that ate part of the woman were simply hungry. They didn't have a meeting before she died to decide who would get the ears and who would get the nose.

When you are dead, you won't have any more awareness of your body. Your spirit will move on to another plane of existence or possibly be devoured by Cthulhu. If Tabby does indeed decide to eat your face, it would only be to sustain the feline's life. If you truly care about the cat, should you not be concerned for his well-being over the condition of a corpse for which you will have no further use? Truthfully, it makes you seem whiny and selfish.

Dear Cthulhu,

I have marital problems. My wife and I've been married for 21 years and were happily married for the first 10 or so. Then we started to grow apart. I can't place the blame for it on either one of us. As we grew more distant, neither one of us really did anything about it. It got to the point where we weren't intimate for a number of years and I decided to talk to a lawyer about what I would have to do to get divorced. There's a lot involved, most important of which would be I'd lose half of my assets. Plus, my wife makes more money than I do, so I'd have to get used to a lower standard of living if we split. I'm not sure if alimony would be enough to make up the difference.

Still, going without sex for so long was making me crazy and I was looking for some shot at getting some. Yes, I know I could just have an affair, but I'm old-fashioned. I would be hurt if she did that to me, so it would be better to divorce her than sleep around on her.

Then everything changed on Halloween. We were invited to a costume party. I went to one of those party stores and picked out an Elvis costume. My wife picked out a Marilyn Monroe outfit and wig. Not that she looked like Marilyn. I mean, we're both middle-aged. And in all fairness, I was in about the same shape as the fat era Elvis rather than the hot, young Elvis.

Since my wife got the Marilyn wig, I decided to get an Elvis style haircut. I had a beard, so I just shaved everything except the sideburns, dyed everything black, and gave myself a pompadour. Then I put on the sequined white jumpsuit, a white scarf, and a pair of sunglasses. My wife and I were both coming from work so we decided to meet at the party.

My wife was already at the party when I got there. She gave me a look up and down like she was starving and I was a T-bone steak. Then she kissed me more passionately than she had in a decade.

"I really like your costume," she told me. Then she started

holding my hand and coming on to me like she did when we first started dating.

Part of the entertainment at the party was a karaoke machine. I don't mean to brag, but I've got a pretty good voice. I had the lead in a few musicals back in high school and I was in a band in college.

Our host insisted I get up and sing. I had no problem with it. I always liked performing in front of an audience. It helped that they were drunk. Intoxicated people are a lot easier to impress than sober ones.

I got up in front of everyone and did *Hunk of Burning Love*, complete with the hip wiggling and the lip thing.

Everybody clapped and when I moved down so the next person could have a turn, someone grabbed me from behind and pulled me into a bedroom, threw me down on a pile of coats on the bed, and started kissing me like it the start of a dirty movie.

Imagine my surprise when I realized it was my own wife. I'd never seen her like this. She tore open my jumpsuit and rode me like I was a horse. I have to admit, it was amazing.

When we were done, she got up and left me alone. She seemed almost embarrassed. She pretty much ignored me for the next hour and a half until our host got me up to do another karaoke number.

This time I did *Jailhouse Rock*. Again, when I was done my wife grabbed me and this time dragged me into a closet on the second floor. She leaned forward and whispered in my ear, "Elvis, I'm your prisoner of love." Then she did things to me that she'd never done before.

I slept well that night. I figured our marriage was at a new turning point and things were going to get better, but the next day she went back to ignoring me. She had about as much interest in me as she did the couch. Less, as she sat on the couch.

I tried to re-create what we had the night before, but every time I touched her she'd just push me away. I was disappointed and figured it probably happened just because she was drunk. So being a guy, I tried to get her drunk again. She fell asleep on me.

The next day it dawned on me. I'd gone back to wearing my hair the old way and the black hair dye was the kind that came out after a few washes. I decided to try an experiment. That Friday night I bought a karaoke machine, re-dyed my hair – this time with the permanent kind – and put on the jumpsuit and sunglasses. I waited in the living room until I heard her car in the driveway.

As soon as I heard her come in and shut the door behind her, I started singing *Hound Dog*. She stood in the doorway of the living room staring at me for a moment, then dropped her briefcase and rushed at me, screaming like she was a groupie.

I tossed her the white scarf and she put it to her face, swooned, and fell to the floor. I stopped singing and made a crack about her coming back with me to the jungle room. We didn't make it that far.

For the next few weeks, it worked out perfectly. Whenever I was in the mood, I threw on the jumpsuit and fired up the karaoke machine. It was amazing. She let me do things that I had asked, even begged, to try before, but the answer had always been no.

Then things took a turn for the worse. She stopped calling me by my real name, and only addressed me as Elvis or King. She didn't need the songs anymore to get worked up. In fact, she bought me a whole new wardrobe and insisted I wear it, each piece representing Elvis from a different era or movie.

She was as insatiable as a horny teenager. I'm 55 years old and she was expecting me to take care of her morning, noon, and night. And even more on the weekends. I had to get prescription pills from my doctor to keep up, if you catch my drift.

I finally sat her down and had a talk, telling her that I was going back to dressing the way I used to, get a crew cut, and let my hair go back to being brown and grey. She grabbed the steak knife and held it to my throat and told me that if I did anything to make Elvis go away she'd kill me. I believed her and started sleeping in the jumpsuit just to be on the safe side.

I can't take it anymore. I feel like her insatiable urges are going to kill me or give me a heart attack.

I realize that if I try to divorce her, she will kill me but I can't go on like this much longer. I tried singing *Don't be Cruel* but she just jumped me instead. What can I do?

– The Once and Fearful King

Dear Fearful,

Sometimes human males annoy me. You started out your letter whining that you wanted to divorce your wife because you were not getting any procreation, then go on to tell me that you are now getting too much. It's obvious that your wife has an obsessive fixation with this pop icon. Instead of looking at this as a chore, you should consider turning it to your advantage. Stop thinking of her as your wife and start treating her like a rock star's groupie. You said that the woman will do anything for you when you're dressed up so do your best to fulfill all your wildest procreation fantasies. Then start making demands. Tell your wife that the King won't put on a performance of any kind until you get something you want done. You could literally live like a king.

And when the pace of procreation becomes too much, simply pull a page out of the King's playbook and tell her Elvis has left the building.

Explain to her that you're going on tour or making a movie and you should get some alone time.

Turn an extra room in your house into a dressing room and put a big star on the door. Tell her that she is not allowed in your dressing room at any time. Don't give in to her every demand. Like I said above, make her work for it. Simply take vacations when you need to in your dressing room. Insist on a big screen TV, surround sound, streaming, a video game system, and a refrigerator filled with food and beverages of your choice. Do this and instead of being her procreation toy, she'll become yours.

Dear Cthulhu,

I recently watched some old black and white movies about PIs and gangsters. I thought it was a pretty cool look so I went up to my vintage clothing store and bought myself a Fedora and a trench coat and started wearing them.

I was expecting a lot of compliments on my new look, maybe even to start a trend bring the old look back. All I got was people making fun of me. I was hoping for a cool new nickname like Bogey but instead, people started calling me grandpa. Then it got shortened and now, despite the fact that I am 20 years old, everybody calls me Gramps.

Cthulhu, what's wrong with people?

– Bogey from Boca Raton

Dear Boca Raton,

Cthulhu is writing a column here, not a doctoral dissertation. Listing everything that was wrong with humanity would take volumes. Instead, how about we start with what's wrong with you? You saw an old movie made before your parents were born and thought it was cool so you decided to play dress up.

There is nothing wrong with that if you had owned it. Instead, you expected one action to suddenly make you hugely popular with people who really don't care about you. In fact, the people that do care about you are probably a very small number. You do not have the chops to be cool on your own so decided to knock off a look that went out more than half a century ago.

Do not worry so much about what other people think or say about you. Be happy with yourself because what you think of yourself is really the only thing that matters in the long run, besides the great Cthulhu, of course. If you like the look, keep it. Or update it. Or learn how to make your own clothes. Take a course in haberdashery and learn how to make your own hats. Use different materials and colors. Pair them with more modern clothes. Save the trench coats for when it's raining. Wear it because it makes you happy, not because you think other people will like you more.

And regarding the name Gramps. It sounds like it has stuck so own that too. Smile a lot and carry butterscotch in your pocket to hand out to people.

Dear Cthulhu,

I'm a huge fan of musicals. Even as a freshman in high school, I managed to snag a lead. Not a year has gone by since then that I haven't been in at least one. I even moved to Manhattan for a while and tried out for Broadway. I made the chorus in a couple shows but being one of the crowd just wasn't my dream.

I needed to be the star, to have my voice ring out in the darkness as a beacon to others. I'll admit my mind did have some trouble processing why I wasn't being given any leads on Broadway.

But then it came – my big break. The lead in a Broadway musical I was in the chorus of didn't show up one night and the understudy was nowhere to be found. It was like 42nd Street. I was in the right place at the right time. I stepped up to take the lead in one of my favorite shows of all time – *The Sound of My Fair Hamilton's Wicked Westside Cats Chorus Line On The Roof*. I was determined to give a performance like none the Great White Way had ever seen before. And despite what the critics may have said, I think I succeeded. I mean, who says the female lead actually has to be played by a woman?

True, there was some small pushback from the director and producers as I stepped out on the stage. Although that was probably only due to the fact that they hadn't asked me to actually play the part but I knew that I would change their minds.

I think the first act went well. The crowd was amused by the novelty of a man in the lead role but then it all came crashing down in act two. And it was all my fault.

Looking back, it never would've happened had I just listened to my mother and became an eye doctor. That way I would've correctly dosed the sleeping pill that I ground up into the drinks I gave to the lead and her understudy and the two would've slept through the entire show instead of waking up and rushing to the theater to rat me out. I mean really – she'd been playing the part for months. You think she wouldn't throw such a hissy fit just because someone else was doing the part once. Plus, I figured she owed me. After all, I paid for the drinks.

The story came out, the director ordered me off the stage, but I refuse to leave. It was my chance in the spotlight and I wasn't giving it up for anyone or anything.

It being Broadway, they weren't about to stop the show for any reason, so they tried creative ways to herd me offstage, but it didn't work. At one point I was left alone on stage dancing in a number I wasn't even supposed to be in. I broke into *The Impossible Dream*. I knew it was from the wrong show, but I thought it might emotionally put the audience in my corner. Just as I was trying to reach that unreachable star, policeman dressed in costume came out and surrounded me, but I hadn't taken twenty years of dance for nothing. I moved like a leaf on the wind, spinning and dodging every flatfoot. They couldn't lay a hand on me.

Unfortunately, they were able to Taser me. But even as I went down, I went down singing. I only pray the audience forgave my voice cracking as the electricity surged through my body.

I was arraigned later that night and tried to explain to the judge in song why I'd done what I had done and why I should be set free.

I must say the results were disappointing. Not my singing, mind you. That was spot on, but not one other person in the courtroom joined in. Nobody got up and danced or sang with me – not the observers, the jury, the lawyers, or the bailiffs. That's the part I find truly unforgivable.

Just because I choose to sing instead of speak, the judge deemed me mentally incompetent and remanded me to Bellevue.

The producers are now stating they would be willing to drop the charges on one condition.

Several of the theatergoers recorded my performance on their cell phones and put the videos up on MeTube. Several of them went viral, particularly my breath control while being

Tasered. The play was scheduled to close in a month. Now, ticket sales are through the roof. But do they thank me by offering me the part again? No. Instead, they simply offered to drop all the charges if I was willing to give up my membership in the Actor's Equity Association. It means that I would never again be able to sing on Broadway.

I simply cannot imagine a life where I do not get to perform on the Great White Way. I simply cannot consider demeaning myself by doing dinner theater in Hoboken.

Should I serve my time in the loony bin and then try to parlay my fifteen minutes of fame into another shot on Broadway when I get out? Can I sue the producers for capitalizing on what I did and maybe get a piece of the action?

– Give My Regards to Broadway

Dear Regards,

Before Cthulhu sat down to give you your answer, he first went on the Internet to watch the videos of your performance. While you do have some singing talent, you simply did not have the stage presence necessary to carry off a lead in a successful Broadway show. Of course, these days, when ticket sales are dipping they have been known to put a celebrity in the cast in order to get more people in the seats. Toward this end, someone who had a viral video might fit the bill. Unfortunately, I would not say your videos went viral. The one of you being Tasered barely got 200,000 hits and none of the others broke 50,000. A true viral video needs well over 1 million hits. And before you sit down at a computer to watch it 800,000 more times, Cthulhu should mention that the video sites have measures in place that stop counting views from the same IP address after about 10 times.

As for your other question, Cthulhu is not an attorney. There are depths to which even I will not sink. However, it is my understanding that in America, anyone can sue anyone else for any reason. Whether or not a court deems your case to have any redeeming merit is another matter. It would appear to me that you have none.

From your written rant, Cthulhu would recommend that you do not give up your union card. It appears to be something which is of great psychological value to you so do not let them take it away. Do your time in the psychiatric ward. Keep in practice by organizing shows with the other patients and when you get out once again find work. Do not be so quick to dismiss dinner theater. Perhaps you would be able to find a producer to let you do a one-man show, or even a traditional musical and have you do all the parts. Would that not that be better than merely having the lead, but being the entire show? In order to fill some seats, use your tiny fame. Another good part about being acting in dinner theater is at least you know where your next meal is coming from.

Dear Cthulhu,

I go to a big beautiful church with thousands of other people every week. The sermons are inspiring and the music is like a concert. Preacher's always going on about how important it is for us to give to him and that we do that to show how much we appreciate God. In return, God will give us even more money. Now I'm only a 16-year-old girl but that sounds fishy to me. My mom's been on her own since my dad ran off with the cashier from the Jiffy Queen and she doesn't make much money but she gives a lot of it to Preacher. It gets to the point sometimes where we have to eat Ramen noodles and peanut butter and jelly sandwiches an awful lot. But we could eat regular food if she didn't give Preacher all that money.

Recently a tornado hit our town and left about fifty people homeless. Our church has convention facilities and a lot of rooms for when people come to visit. I know from helping my mom clean up the place that Preacher could put up half, maybe even all those people in their own room with a bed without any problem.

Preacher's always going on about how the Bible tells us we're supposed to help least of our brothers and he claims that he uses some of our money to send the word of God by his Internet show into prisons and nursing homes in Third World countries. Sadly, that appears to be the extent of his help.

Meanwhile, he doesn't send them anything in terms of food or clothing or other necessities, while he's got a fifty thousand dollar car and a mansion with a big gate around it. When I asked him if he'd put up those people he told me that's not what God wants. I think he's full of bulldookie.

I think what Preacher is preaching is a very good thing. Helping others and being good to people is what life is all about and I think most of the people who go to our church do what they're supposed to. Preacher, on the other hand, is not practicing what he preaches.

I don't think my mama should be giving money to somebody who's saying one thing and doing another but how do I get her to stop giving him so much money?

– Believer Tired of Being Bamboozled in Biloxi

Dear Biloxi,

For someone of such a young age, Cthulhu thinks you are doing a good job of perceiving the dishonesty in your species.

The truth of the matter is there are a lot of people out there who are more than willing to take advantage of their fellow humans in order to advance their own lives. Money is one of the most reasons for it. It sounds like your preachers also getting a bit in the prestige and power department as well. The sad and simple truth of the matter is when most people give to someone like your preacher, it doesn't matter what they do with the donation because they believe and have faith in him instead of in the higher power that he serves.

This would never happen in the Cult of Cthulhu because all of my reverends know that all worship must be directed only at Cthulhu and there are severe consequences if it happens otherwise. Your church is not so blessed, so feel free to consider converting if you want to avoid this in the future.

Also, your mother likely views you as just a child which means she will most likely not listen to what you have to say. But do not be too harsh on her. She thinks she is doing a good thing and buying blessings for her family by doing this. Direct confrontation with you and your mother or you and the preacher won't get you anywhere. Truthfully the best bet is when you are older tell you simply to change a place of worship that more suits your beliefs but that is not an option now as you are still a minor.

Your best option to change this situation is to post anonymously on social media and question why such a prosperous preacher did not step up to help those in his town who needed it. Hopefully, the Internet will shame him and maybe force him to do the right thing. Maybe during that shame, you could so some spin doctoring of your own. Approach him and mentioned the poverty that your own family is facing and tell him that you had reporters from network TV talking to you about it and that you mentioned to them how much money your mother gives the church and how many problems you're having with not having enough food and such. Then mention that they wanted to see if why he wasn't doing anything to help your family so you came to him to ask. Tell him they said they would check back in with you soon. In order to get good PR, he might just get your family some of the things that you need.

Dear Cthulhu,

My kids are five and six years old and their father and I recently divorced. He ran off with our milk woman. Although truth be told I'm not sure if she actually was a milk woman or if that was the story they made up when I came home early one day caught her in our kitchen helping herself to the milk in our refrigerator. I honestly don't think there are any working dairy delivery people anymore.

Anyway, it was a tough time for both me and the kids and they had been wanting a dog. I broke down and got them a puppy. They named him Rags. They loved this dog and he was a mutt with all sorts of unique spots and markings unlike anything I've ever seen before. They didn't want to leave him long enough to go to school so I brought Rags in the car when I dropped them off at school. Then I took him home before I went to work.

One morning after the kids got off okay, I rushed home so I could drop the puppy off and still make it to work on time. Rags was in the front passenger seat with his paws up on the door and his little head hanging out the window. Because he was such a small thing, when I hit a pothole on the highway poor Rags got thrown out the window. Rags was wearing his leash which was hooked on the emergency brake. I thought it was short enough to make sure he stayed in the car, but I misjudged. The poor thing fell out the window and his neck snapped, killing him instantly.

I called in sick to work and tried to find another puppy that looked just like Rags but like I said he was pretty unique and I couldn't do it.

So when I picked the kids up at school, I had to tell them that Rags ran away. I may have bitterly added under my breath that he probably ran off with the milk woman.

I didn't realize the kids heard me until the next visitation with her father when they accused his slut of stealing their dog and told her she had to give Rags back.

It's caused quite the rift with their father and his dairy whore.

I don't know if I should come clean and tell the kids he died because we've been going out every day to look for him and have posted lost dog posters on every telephone pole in town. I even offered to get them a new puppy but they said they didn't want to so Rags wouldn't be upset when he came back.

What should I do?

-Mama Dog-mangler in Matilda

Dear Matilda,

You are the parent and that means you are in charge. Tell your offspring that you got a notice from the police that the dog died. You didn't mention what you did with the body but if you can still get a hold of it, give the children closure and bury the pet in the backyard. If you can't, burn something and put in an urn and tell them it is Rags. Dump the ashes in your backyard, have a little service, and move on.

If they still want, get them a new puppy. It sounds like you did not have the first one long so within a month your offspring will be just as happy with it. Although from now on drive with the windows closed and the doors locked when the dog is in the car.

Dear Cthulhu,

I'm an old-school kind of guy. I grew up on a farm. All my neighbors heat their homes with gas, electric, or oil but I use a wood stove. In my opinion, it's far superior to the other methods and keeps my house warmer too. Plus, I chop my own wood which keeps me in pretty good shape. The problem is I grew up in the country and we were able to go out into the woods and chop down trees on my family farm and use that to heat our house growing up. Farming wasn't for me so I moved to the suburbs where there simply aren't any woods.

When I first moved here, I'd go spend a weekend at the farm, chop down a tree, use a chainsaw and the wood splitter and fill up my pickup truck. I'd get enough wood to heat my house for months.

And not only was my woodstove the superior house heating method, it was free. Unfortunately, my parents decided that after more than 40 years of farming it was time for them to retire. They offered the farm to me and my siblings but we'd all had our fill farming growing up and decided to go on to other things. Someone else bought the family homestead and suddenly I was cut off from my wood supply.

I tried to spread out my remaining wood but eventually, it ran out. I broke down and actually went out looking to buy some would but to my surprise in suburbia, wood is generally sold in very small bundles and is ridiculously expensive. I finally figured out why my neighbors didn't heat their houses with it – without a free supply, it's expensive. I looked into converting my house to gas oil and electric but it would cost me thousands of dollars. I've got a decent job but money is tight. I picked the house I did because of the wood stove. By the time I'm done paying my mortgage cable, cell phone, internet, and my pickup truck payment, I'm left with enough for groceries and that's it. I was always taught that credit cards were bad because you didn't want to spend money you didn't have and drag yourself down into never-ending debt.

Instead, I came up with a different solution. I work four ten hour days at my job which means I have Tuesdays off. I throw on a pair of overalls and a hard hat. I've got a magnetic sign on my truck that says that I work for the local power company. I go around to my neighbors on blocks where nobody is home and use my chainsaw to chop down random trees, then cut them up and load them into my pickup truck. Because I'm afraid of getting caught I tend to pick trees around the small to medium-size so the wood only lasts me a few weeks each time.

It turns out that sneaking around people's backyards and chopping down their trees upsets them. The people I did the free landscaping for called the cops. Believe it or not, it's apparently illegal to chop down people's trees without their permission. Must've been a quiet news cycle, because I ended up making the TV news and even got a nickname – the Wood Bandit.

According to the news stories, the police are keeping an eye out for me and there is even a small reward for information leading to my arrest and conviction. It's got me so worried I haven't gone out to replenish my firewood supply so I've got maybe two weeks of wood left and they're saying it's going to be a long winter. I don't want to live in a cold house or have my pipes freeze and burst.

I'm thinking of maybe driving to another town and trying it there but I don't know how far the story spread. I don't want to get caught and lose my job and my house.

What can I do?

– Wood Taker in Woodburn

Dear Woodburn,

There are many different options available to you. Cthulhu has heard of people who take newspapers, roll them up and burn them instead of wood. If Tuesday is your town's recycling day, drive around and take newspapers from your neighborhood's recycling bin and try and use them. It is usually not illegal to take things out of someone's garbage and recycling may fall into that same category. However, Cthulhu is not sure how efficient that would be.

Go around after a storm and pick up larger limbs of trees that have fallen. You could follow around the actual powerline crews if they cut the trees around the power lines in your town and take the wood that they cut down.

There is another option available that would probably be the better solution. You say you grew up in the country and it was close enough for you to drive to chop down a tree and prepare the wood over a weekend. A lot of rural areas have hunting clubs. For many of these clubs, one of the benefits involves being able to go onto their property and cut down trees to use at your home for firewood. It would involve paying a membership fee but it would likely be much less expensive than buying the wood in your town or going to jail.

Another possibility is to open a tree removal business. Make some phone calls and see what other similar companies charge and set your prices significantly lower. That way when a tree comes down people will call you to come remove it. That way not only do you get the wood you need to heat your house, but you can get some extra cash in the process.

Dear Cthulhu,

I live to play golf. I work to have money to support my wife and kids who I adore but if my wife ever tried to stop me from playing golf I'd divorce her in a second.

I'm also very competitive. I've played in several semipro tournaments and did very well. My boss knows how much I love golf so if I make quota for the month he lets me leave an hour early on the first workday of the next month to go play. He even covers the tab for eighteen holes.

Of course, he does the same thing for the other salesman. Last month only Joe and I made quota so were the only ones who got to go golfing. The course is next to some people's property and I hit the ball over their fence.

I didn't want to take the one-stroke penalty so I hopped the fence, intending to hit my ball back on the course. What I didn't count on was the people had a dog and while I was swinging, he came at me. I didn't even see the dog but as I brought my swing back I smashed him in the head an instant before he tore into my ankle.

The fleabag messed up my shot and my ball didn't make it over the fence. Oh, and I hit him so hard that he died.

I tried again and this time hit the ball through the links in the fence. I climbed back over onto the course and finished the hold one over par. I realize I probably should've come clean and told the dog's owners what happened, but technically I was trespassing and people are crazy about their animals.

If the story about me beating a dog to death with my golf club hit the papers, my days as a salesman would be over so I kept my mouth shut.

Unfortunately, Joe saw the whole thing and we reached the eighteenth hole, he told me that if I didn't tell everyone at work that he beat me by ten strokes that he'd squeal and tell everybody what happened.

Ten strokes was ridiculous. Joe's beaten me maybe once in

the last three years and that was because I had the flu and was playing with a 102-degree temperature. First, I didn't have a better option, so I agreed to it. Now Joe wants to go golfing with me all the time and is making me tell people he's beating me left and right. It's embarrassing. It's gotten to the point where I am debating about going up to the people's door and throwing myself on the mercy.

What should I do, Cthulhu?

– Golfer in Georgia

Dear Georgia,

Honesty may not be the best policy, but sometimes it turns out to be better than the alternative. You are obviously having issues giving up dominance in your game to your coworker so you have to come up with some way to counter his blackmail. You could go confess and throw yourself on the mercy of the dog's owners or you could tell Joe that you were going to go and tell them that he did it.

In a case like this it's he said versus he said. If you both stick to your stories there shouldn't be enough evidence against either of you for charges to be placed so long as you are smart and get rid of your club in such a way that it will never be traced back to you as the dog could have left tissue or blood residue there.

While it might be tempting to plant the club on your co-worker's property, if he does not have the same set of clubs as you do, it will backfire and it will point back to you.

While it would be unusual to expend the time, effort, and money to do this if you get somebody in law enforcement who is an animal lover they might go the extra mile. Replace the club with an exact replica by going to someplace far away and paying cash for it. This way no one will be suspicious about a missing club and if you don't replace it, the club's absence will lend more credence to your co-worker's story.

The simple truth of the matter is if you're threatening him and he's threatening you, your co-worker will likely not push it any further.

Dear Cthulhu,

I would call my daughter a whore or a slut, but those terms don't even begin to describe her. She has seven different children by ten different fathers. No, I didn't write that wrong. She apparently nailed three guys at different times in a bar on the same night and told all three of them that they're the boy's father. They must believe her, as all three of them pay child support. And as horrible a daughter as she is, she makes an even worse mother. She gets a fortune in child support payments and a few monthly blackmail payments because of some videos she made but she doesn't spend a dime of it on her children.

In fact, she doesn't even spend any time with them. She just pops them out and dumps them on my doorstep, expecting me to take care of them. Of course, they're my flesh and blood so I do. It's not like I can turn them out on the street. The problem is, I'm older and still working full time. I don't have the strength or the energy to be raising seven children. Nor can I really afford it. I can't even apply for welfare or food stamps for them because I'm technically not their legal guardian. Slutty McLoosepants is. I have no time for myself. And even if I did have time, after feeding and clothing seven children. I have no money left to do anything fun. I raised my kids. How do I get Slutty McLoosepants to do the same with hers?

– Grandmother At Her Wit's End in Wichita

Dear Grandmother,

You cannot blame this entire situation on your offspring with loose morals. No one can take advantage of you without your consent.

The first time she dumped a baby on your doorstep, you should've laid down the law and told her it was not your job to raise her children, although you could offer to babysit on occasion.

Because you've let this go on for so long, an ultimatum at this point is unlikely to change her behavior, but giving her one and then following through on it is the only way this is going to change. You claim that you care about your grandchildren, yet you want to turn them over to a woman who, by your own admission, is a horrible mother. This does not sound like the best thing for these tiny humans. Instead, consider demanding that she pay you child support for taking care of her offspring. And spend time away from them to give you more time to yourself. This would solve your two major complaints as you would have more money and some time to yourself.

However, if you do not find this outcome acceptable, then forget the ultimatums and simply bring the young ones to her residence and drop them off with their things. Tell your daughter that you've had enough and it is up to her to take care of these children. However, it does not sound likely that she will suddenly change your ways so you will probably need to monitor the welfare of the children. If it gets too bad, you will likely have to report her to child protective services and a government agency will do the raising of what you call your flesh and blood for you. True, the children will likely end up in separate foster homes but it will not be your problem any longer.

If you decide to keep them and are unsuccessful in getting any support payments or babysitting services, you might want to take her aside and explain to her how these children are made and methods she can use to prevent that from happening. Human doctors can implant something to prevent her from having more children, but this is not foolproof. I suggest you offer her as a birthday gift the opportunity to have her neutered. This way she can go out and procreate to her heart's – or other body parts – content and you will not have to worry about taking care of the consequences of any of those encounters.

Or you can simply drop off the little ones at the nearest Cult of Cthulhu temple where they will be well cared for. At least until suppertime.

Dear Cthulhu,

My wife is a nymphomaniac. I didn't mind all the attention until I found out that she was cheating on me several times a day with different men.

I told the whore I wanted a divorce and she told me that was fine but she'd take half of everything I have. Which is a lot because I'm wealthy. Then I reminded her that she had signed a prenup that states that if she's unfaithful she gets nothing. Which shouldn't really be in a problem proving in court since I found out about her cheating by watching a video of her with an entire men's softball team.

Now she's countersuing me saying that the prenup should be null and void because I'm being discriminatory against her and violating the Americans with Disabilities Act because she's not a nymphomaniac, but a sex addict. She claims I should pay for her to go to rehab to get "cured". I figured this was total nonsense, but my attorneys say that, depending on the judge, things might be ruled her way. Not because of some legal precedent, but because she showed up at a meeting of the local judiciary society and slept with most of the judges. My lawyer feels that this might exert some undue influence over their decision, either out of sentiment or blackmail.

I don't think I should lose half of everything I own because my wife's a slut. What should I do?

– Soon-To-Be Ex-Husband of a Super-Slut

Dear Soon,

Cthulhu is not a lawyer. Despite what you may have heard about where I lay dreaming, there are some depths to which even I will not dive. However, it seems to me that on the legal merits alone, she does not have a case. The Americans with Disabilities Act has a fairly narrow system of classification for which this does not qualify. It states that certain mental impairments are explicitly excluded, including sexual behavior disorders, compulsive gambling, kleptomania, and pyromania. Of course, in your country that would not stop her from suing.

There seems to be a simple way to handle, one that your lawyer should have thought of on their own. Get a list of the jurists who were at that meeting and assume she procreated with them all. Should any of them be chosen for her case insist they recuse themselves. Most will rather than risking exposure. Or better yet insist on a female judge who'll be more likely to rule on the merits of the case as opposed to past episodes of procreation with your former bride.

Dear Cthulhu,

I read the letter from Paranoid of a Tabby in Tacoma and was writing to correct an error. I was Susie's other stalker. I was in the same boat as Paranoid, following Susie around but not having the courage to actually speak to her. In the end, I didn't have Paranoid's patience. After three weeks, I decided it was time for us to meet. It did not go well.

I don't understand why. I brought her chocolate and flowers. Perhaps it was my timing. She didn't appear to appreciate being woken up in her bed at 2:15 in the morning. Susie was even less appreciative of the fact that I had tied her hands and feet to the bed frame before waking her.

I did my best to convince her that we were destined to be together. She rejected my love, told me to get out of her apartment and go to hell.

That was not how that moment was supposed to go. Susie was supposed to tell me that she'd been waiting for me her whole life and that she loved me even more than I love her. She should have told me that we were going to be together forever.

Well, she screwed that perfect moment up and I don't take rejection well so I kind of accidentally strangled her for 45 minutes. Unfortunately, after that she was dead and I couldn't convince her that she was wrong to reject me. Not that I didn't try to make her. I used her as a puppet and tried to make her say the words I wanted to hear. But it turns out I suck as a ventriloquist and even I wasn't convinced. There was no sincerity to it and the voice was too high and screechy.

Since I couldn't kill her again I needed to do something to help me feel better after such harsh rejection so I tried to kill her cats too but they weren't having any of it. The buggers hid from me, so I hid all the cat food in the house and rubbed tuna fish all over Susie's face.

It took three days before they did chow down and it took a lot of work on my part. But what they say about really appreciating something you worked hard for is true. Getting them to eat her face off gave me a great feeling of satisfaction because I knew somewhere Susie was really regretting having rejected me.

Unfortunately, I stayed in the apartment too long and her dead body started to really sink. So did the litter box because I wasn't about to clean it. Her neighbors called the cops and they arrested me. I can't afford a lawyer so I get a public defender and he suggested I take a plea deal that would make me eligible for parole in twenty years. I think I can beat this if I just explained to the jury that the whole mess was Susie's own fault for not loving me like she was supposed to. Do you think that would be the best way to go?

Oh and tell Paranoid that he was lucky not to have to deal with such a fickle woman.

-The Real Stalker in Tacoma

Dear Real,

Only you can decide what is the best decision for you when it comes to the legal system. I would like to again state two things – one Cthulhu is not a lawyer and two, humans should not kill humans. That is the prerogative of great Cthulhu only. You should not damage what will one day be my property.

Still, from what I know of the human justice system in your country, the jury will not be swayed by your words and you may end up getting a harsher sentence. Taking the deal lets you off much lighter than you would be if Cthulhu were to decide your sentence.

Dear Cthulhu,

I wrote to you a while back after trying to hijack the lead in a Broadway show by drugging the lead and her understudy and playing the female lead despite being a man.

As I mentioned in my last letter, I ended up in Bellevue. The producers eventually ended up dropping the charges and I was set free. I tried to return to acting upon the stage, but alas it was not to be. Word of what I had done had gotten around to all the casting directors and I could not find work, even in a traveling roadshow. I'd say I couldn't get arrested in this town, but alas that is not sure.

I took this blow to my career right quite grievously. Many of the other greats turned to booze and drugs in their dark days but I did not.

I still had my magnificent voice and I knew deep in my heart of hearts that the public wanted to hear me sing. At first, I tried to capitalize upon my fame on the Internet for the video of me being Tasered yet fighting on to continue to sing upon the stage. I put up videos of me singing classic show tunes, but I simply did not get enough people viewing. In fact, the last one I put up only got twelve hits, at least ten of which were from me.

I still had to eat, so I lowered myself to take a job doing singing telegrams. For the first week or so it worked out marvelously. The simple truth of the matter was people with my range and quality of voice simply do not do singing telegrams, so the recipients of my songs were overwhelmed and brought to tears by my voice. Although one woman claimed the tears were because I would not leave.

I will admit to having some trouble with my material. Many of the telegrams were written by the people who were paying to send them and they were utter drivel. Think of kindergarteners trying to write a poem –

Roses are red,

Violets are blue,
Your butt is sweet,
I want to do you.

Others were worse, as if the kindergartener's poem was run through a shredder along with other random documents and pasted back together by a blind crack addict

Having had to listen to such drivel, I felt the customer should get a treat. So after I finished a telegram, I'd do a medley of show tunes. Just some well-known favorites. I always promised myself to keep it under an hour, unless of course an encore was demanded. It never was.

But even that menial job is now lost to me, although perhaps fate played no small part in that. I was hired to deliver a singing telegram to a bat mitzvah, the Jewish ceremony when a girl becomes a woman. I was to sing the song her father wrote, then I planned to sing a medley of songs dedicated to the joys of becoming a woman.

But I went to the wrong room at the catering hall. It turns out a group of transgender people had rented it across from the bat mitzvah to pay tribute to a friend who was killed by anesthesia during a gender reassignment surgery. When they heard my songs, they went wild and tried to kill me. Once again my dance training came in handy and allowed me to spin and nobody could touch me on the dance floor. I almost got away, but only almost. One of the guests who had negative experiences with gay bashing in the past had taken to carrying her own Taser and, once again, thunderbolts were unleashed upon me. And once again I did not stop singing as surging electricity brought me down.

More's the pity that it wasn't recorded because this one would've broken a million hits for sure.

As an unemployed actor, I have no health insurance and it seems likely I will be needing a few months of rehab after my beating after the Taser attack. Are those that beat me responsible for my medical bills? And the father of the 13-year-old girl I was supposed to sing to refused to pay because I never delivered the telegram to its proper recipient. But I have a copy of the contract which states clearly to go to ballroom B, where the memorial service was being held. Since I did as instructed, aren't I entitled to that hundred dollars?

I threatened to press charges against my attackers if they didn't pay my medical bills, but then they threatened to have me charged with a hate crime for what I did. I want to explain to them that I really didn't do anything. I don't care about anyone's sexual orientation or what gender they are. The only thing I care about is that they like my singing. For crying out loud, in my swansong on Broadway, I was performing as a woman. I don't hate anyone. All I wanted to do was bring a little extra cheer to little girl's special day. I even starred in La Cage aux Folles in high school. These charges are ridiculous.

Cthulhu, what can I do?

– Still Trying To Give My Regards To Broadway But Broadway's Not Returning My Calls.

Dear Regards,

You might as well plead your case to your attackers, preferably over the phone.

A sensible option would be to speak to a social worker at the hospital you are in and explain your situation to them. There are programs in place such as Medicaid which can help those who don't have the financial ability to pay for medical care. The hospital will go out of its way to help you qualify for these programs because they know without them, they are likely to go unpaid.

As for whether or not you are owed the hundred dollars, it could be argued successfully by an attorney that because you followed the instructions you were given, you should be paid. In fact, a skilled attorney might be able to make a case that your injuries and pain and suffering were due to him giving you instructions and might be able to get a settlement.

Dear Cthulhu,

I'm a dairy farmer who recently had a bunch of no good, stupid teenagers come on my property with the intention of tipping my cows. These morons were drunk and got into a field with my prize bull, who tore up one of the poor kids. Thankfully, his parents have decided not to sue me, realizing their son was at fault. However, his friends are now suing me over having been traumatized by watching the bull kill their friend.

This whole lawsuit is utter nonsense. But if they win I could lose the farm. It's been in my family for seven generations. What am I gonna do?

– Frantic Farmer

Dear Frantic,

Despite frequent requests for legal advice, Cthulhu is not a lawyer and has made his opinion of the profession clear many times in the past. Although this is coming up so much lately, Cthulhu is considering taking the bar exam just to be able to charge for his advice. However, typically the best way to deal with a lawsuit is to file a bigger counter lawsuit.

These youths say they were traumatized – you counter that so were you. I assume like most people who live in the country, you have no trespassing signs posted. These teenagers broke the law. You have to live with the fact that a young man was killed on your property and it has been giving you nightmares.

Are you married? Say it has caused marital difficulties. Have your wife temporarily move out and stay with family. You could cite alienation of marital factions as one of the parts of the suit. But perhaps it is not only you that's been traumatized. How is your bull? You say he was a prize bull. This can mean that besides pimping him out for your own cows that you sell his seed to other farmers. You could easily claim that the bull is not able to perform his stud duties with your cows and you are having difficulty getting enough seed to put on the market and that you have had a loss of income.

Have your lawyer add one more zero to your suit than those people suing you.

What will likely end up happening is the lawyers will meet and come up with a solution that seems to benefit you, but benefits them far more as they will get a third of any damages collected. They will come out with some much smaller number that with any luck you will be able to get your insurance company to pay for you. You'll end up with a small increase in premium but should be able to continue business on your farm.

Dear Cthulhu,

My wife and I been married five years and in that time my mother-in-law and I have never gotten along at all

Lately, that's been affecting my marriage because my wife has been taking her mother's side in most of our disagreements. Plus, my mother-in-law spends a lot of the time at our house which is cutting into our alone-time together. I've been coping by going out drinking with the guys. To be honest, it's just to get out of the house because there are nights that I don't even actually have so much as a beer.

Last week I came home late and went into my bedroom, stripped down to my underwear and climbed into bed. I had been missing my wife and put my arm around her and spooned her from behind. To be honest, I expected her to slap my arm away like she'd been doing for so long but instead, she pressed back into me and started grinding on me. Before long, we were going at it like a pair of teenagers.

My wife had never been that enthusiastic in bed before. She did things that not only had she never done but I had never even heard of. It was the most amazing night of my life, that is until the morning when I woke up facing my naked mother-in-law, who apparently liked me now.

She liked me so much she gave me a repeat performance of the night before. At first, I tried to resist but she was insistent and my body was weak. I went downstairs for breakfast to see my wife making eggs and bacon. She told me she had given her mother our bedroom for the night and she hoped that I didn't mind sleeping in the guest room next door. I told her it all worked out fine. My mother-in-law came into the kitchen in a robe, flashed me then sat down opposite me and played footsie with me during the whole meal. Now my mother-in-law's been asking me to help with a lot of things around her house and with errands and it's been amazing.

My mother-in-law has been talking me up so now my wife

actually seems to like me again. Sadly, I don't really have any interest in her anymore.

Here's my problem. My wife is suggesting that her mother move in with us, which seems like a great idea. I won't have to constantly be going the five miles to her place. However, it's still a big decision. What do you think?

– Satisfied Son-in-law in Suffolk

Dear Satisfied,

This seems like a very bad idea. First, you are breaking your vows to your wife whom you promised to love, cherish, and procreate with no one but her. Vow breaking is wrong as I've stated many times before. Cthulhu has cultists who have made vows to Cthulhu. If the other humans break vows, they may get the idea that it is okay for them to do so and discipline would take up too much of my time.

There is a far more practical aspect that makes this a bad idea for you. If you and your mother-in-law are in the same house, it is only a matter of time before your wife finds out about your extramarital procreation activities. I cannot imagine this ending well for either of you, so if you're going to continue to vow break you should at least have a place that you can procreate without the risk of discovery.

Dear Cthulhu,

I'm writing after reading the letter from the guy who was being made fun of because he decided to start wearing a Fedora and trench coat. I'm having a similar – yet altogether different – clothing related issue.

I like to wear women's skirts. I don't want to be a woman. I'm heterosexual, like women, and have no interest in other men. I just like the freedom wearing a skirt gives me but the only time I really get to do it is cosplaying at cons and on Halloween because I'm too afraid of what other people will say. I'm worried that because of this I will be stuck in uncomfortable pants forever.

What should I do?

– Afraid and Skirting the Issue In Illinois

Dear Illinois,

Cowardice is a frequent problem with humans. They are so afraid of what others will say to or about them that they spend their whole lives not doing things they want to do. I've been writing this column for over a decade and yet you humans have not learned that the only thing you really need to fear is Cthulhu himself.

As is often the case, there is an easy solution for you. I do not know your ethnic origin and probably couldn't tell by looking at you as all humans look pretty much alike to me, but there are people from Scotland, Ireland, Wales, and other British Isles where men wearing skirts is not seen as a big deal. In fact, for many, it is linked to cultural pride. The only difference is they don't call them skirts, they call them kilts.

In fact, if you are one of these lineages there is likely a pattern for you. There were scam artists back in the 1800s who convinced everyone, including the Queen of England, that there was a centuries-old history and tradition for these kilt patterns that were linked to certain clans and families. This was despite the fact that they made it all up themselves so they could sell kilts.

In the interim, this sham has been accepted as truth and it is now looked upon with great cultural and family pride. If you are not of any of these ethnic backgrounds, you can simply tell people that you used one of these online sites that trace your genealogy and found out that you are Irish or Scottish. In honor of your ancestry, you have decided to start wearing skirts, rather kilts, to get more in touch with your ethnic heritage. In fact, you could even take up playing the drums or the bagpipes and join a group that marches in a St. Patrick's Day parades or such. This would give you a culturally accepted reason to often wear your kilt in public.

Now stop listening to other people and start living your life the way you want to live.

Dear Cthulhu,

I may be the lowest form of scum who has ever written to you. I have a gambling problem. I'll bet on craps, poker, old maid, and any kind of racing from horse to cockroach. I know the odds are stacked against me, but in the heat of the moment, I always think I'm about to make my big score.

Christmas is coming and my wife and I have been putting money into a Christmas club account all year so we can get my three kids the things that they really want for Christmas.

The problem is I made bets on who would win the election. Not the big one for president or anything like that, but the one for dogcatcher. I lost big time and my bookie, Mama Daisy, was unhappy that I hadn't paid up in full and she came over with a couple of leg breakers to convince me to honor my debts. I explained to her that I've been out of work since one of my coworkers bet me I wouldn't punch our boss in the face. That bet I won but I lost my job.

Mama Daisy didn't care. My kneecap was about to be pulverized when I mentioned the Christmas gifts. Mama Daisy's eyes lit up. She was a mother too and each of our three kids had gotten a toy that was now hard to find but was easy when we bought them back in September.

In order to save my kneecap, I gave my kids' Christmas presents to her. Now my wife's going to kick me out and my kids are not going to have any presents for Christmas. I need help. What am I going to do?

– Betting Man in Buffalo

Dear Betting Man,

Humans have a tendency to be weak and self-destructive. Your gambling issues are hurting those you care about the most. The first thing you need to do is get yourself into a 12-step program and man up and do what you know you are supposed to do.

Because so many humans are self-destructive there are other humans with loftier ideals who have put systems in place to help sad ones like you out in times of trouble. There are many organizations who donate Christmas presents to families in need.

There is no guarantee that your children will get the gifts they wanted but some gifts are better than no better than none. Contact them by email pretending to be your wife and tell them the story. By her telling the tale, it should play on the sympathies more so than if you did.

And just to help you with your addiction, I bet you that you can't go for the next 50 years without making another bet. The stakes in this one are your family, so for once in your life do not lose.

Dear Cthulhu,

I've been dating "Nancy" at college for the last six months. She's pretty, smart, and funny. I thought she was the whole package until she took me home for the holiday break to meet her family. They were pretty nice, although I felt pretty bad for her dad as he was the only man in a house of all women including her three sisters, her mother, and even her grandmother. I was amazed that each one of her sisters, and even her mother, were all prettier than she was. Even her grandmother was hot considering she was old.

Nancy comes from an old-fashioned family, so even though we slept together a couple times a day at college, we had to sleep in separate bedrooms.

At some time during the night, I was woken up by a very pleasant sensation and looked down to see the blanket over my pelvis bobbing up and down.

As much as I begged, that wasn't the sort of thing that Nancy liked to do, although she did do it once for my birthday. I didn't know what had gotten into her but I was enjoying it. I've figured maybe it was some sort of forbidden fruit in her parents' house and boy, had her technique improved.

It wasn't long before I exploded and collapsed. By the time I looked up, the bedroom door was closing. That should've been my first clue. Nancy was all about the cuddle.

The next morning when we were alone. I thanked her and she looked at me like a deer in the headlights. She had no idea what I was talking about and said she didn't come see me. I then played it off like it must've been a dream, but I know it wasn't.

We're going back to her house to visit in a few weeks. My question is, how do I figure out which of her family members came to visit me that night? Like I said, each of her three sisters and her mother is way hotter than she is, so I guess I'd be willing to dump her for one of her sisters. If it's the mom, I guess we'd have to carry on a clandestine affair. If it's her grandmother, I guess I might just resign myself to the stolen visits in the middle of the night when I visit. In order to proceed though, I need to figure out which one visited me. How can I do that?

– Got a Naughty Nighttime Visitor in Manitoba

Dear Manitoba,

Without having any video surveillance or having swabbed your nether region for traces of DNA to check against her family members your answer would be difficult to figure out. And since you did not mention any skills in genetic testing, highly impractical.

The truth is, you may never know. Your nighttime visitor could have been a one-time deal. However, there is always the possibility that during your next visit, the experience will repeat itself, at which time you'll have to focus enough past your enjoyment to make a positive identification of your visitor. However, I would like to point out that you left out one possibility. It could be one of the female members of her clan, but it could also be her father. Best make sure you're prepared to consider all possibilities.

Dear Cthulhu,

I've been married to the same woman for 11 years and she's drank heavily for most of them. And before you ask, no, I don't think it's because she's married to me.

A while back she was getting very bad. She was missing work and having blackouts. One time she even woke up in an alleyway wearing a donkey suit. It got so bad that her friends, family, and I staged an intervention and managed to convince her that she had a problem. It worked and she joined AA and has been sober ever since.

That intervention was the worst mistake of my life. My wife may have been a drunk, but at least she was fun. Every day was an adventure and every night a ride on the train of love. Overall, I was a reasonably happy man who worried a bit too much about his drunken wife.

Ever since she sobered up, I've been the worse for wear. "Luscious" has become an uptight nasty woman who's forgotten how to have a good time. She obsesses about every little thing from whether or not the cell phone carrier charged us too much for data to why I was seven minutes later than usual getting home from work. She's made us both take up crocheting. Worst of all, the love train has left the station and is not scheduled to return. Apparently ever. For whatever reason, without alcohol, she no longer wants to make love, kiss, cuddle, or even hug. She prefers a firm, hearty handshake or on special occasions, a peck on the cheek.

Having had a yearly ticket for the love train, I never realized how bad off I would be without it. My wife has done very well in the 12 step program and goes to a meeting every week. I'm actually very proud of that. What I'm not thrilled about is that we don't go out dancing on the front lawn in our underwear anymore.

I take my marriage vows seriously. I still love Luscious, I just don't like her very much. In my darker moments, I've been tempted to slip her a drink, but I can't do that to her. However, I want to get back on the love train. I didn't get married to live a life of celibacy. I thought about sending her the doctor get a prescription but from what I've been told, alcoholics have to be careful to avoid any addicting substance. What can I do to get my fun and sexy wife back?

– Intervenor in Illinois

Dear Intervenor,

The truth of the matter is there are rare humans who function better when under the influence of alcohol or drugs, although they are the exception rather than the rule. It sounds as if your wife may be one of them. This doesn't mean that you should start her back drinking again. Even though she may be more fun and amorous, the long-term effects of alcohol on the human body are not good, particularly in its destruction of the liver.

Going through these recent changes have probably been very stressful for your spouse, especially since she had spent so many years using alcohol as stress relief. You should work with her to find things to do that you both will find enjoyable or fun as well as things that will relieve stress. Procreation is a favorite of many humans, but it sounds as if you will need to work up to that. Exercise is a good way for humans to relieve stress, whether it is running, sports, or even something as simple as yoga. Since your wife is already demonstrated an addictive personality, perhaps you can trade one bad addiction for a healthy one. Try to get her into exercise-related activities in the hopes that her addictive behavior will start kicking in and she may exercise with the same vigor that she used to drink. If she is able to do an activity for twenty minutes or more, the body will release endorphins which will give her a natural high which – while not as intense and long-lasting as alcohol – will probably be better than what she is going through right now.

Instead of being so concerned about the love train, perhaps you should consider bringing the romance back into your relationship. Buy her flowers and perform romantic acts. Offer to give her massages which have also been known to reduce stress and release those same endorphins. Help her out with things around the house because the more you do the less she has to, which will reduce her stress and as time goes by, perhaps you will start to see glimpses of her fun-loving personality start to return.

Dear Cthulhu,

It is my lifelong dream to become a motivational speaker. I can't think of anything better to do with my life than tell other people what they should do and have them pay me lots of money for telling them.

Most motivational speakers start out with nothing, many as losers and then work themselves up to greatness and then share what changed their life with other people to get their payday. I got the first part down. I'm 27 years old and I still live in my parents' basement. I've never held a job for more than a month. It is the achieving greatness part that has eluded me. In my defense, between my playing video games and watching porn on the Internet, there really isn't a lot of time left in my schedule to do anything else.

So I figured who has a bigger following than the Beatles? Cthulhu, of course. If anyone else had to key to motivating millions of people, it's you. So please tell me what I can do to become a motivational speaker who makes millions of dollars so I can buy my own jet to play video games and watch porn in.

– Unmotivated Motivational Speaker in Montana

Dear Unmotivated,

Cthulhu does not have to work to motivate others. One of my many natural gifts is the ability to frighten and terrify people, which is what I find to be the best motivation there is. If someone displeases me, they will die horribly at my tentacles. You would be amazed at how motivating this consequence can be for others.

However, this will not work for you as no human could hope to inspire the same level of fear as Cthulhu.

You make a large and faulty assumption. You think that I will just give you something worth tens if not hundreds of millions of dollars without you giving something of equal value to Cthulhu in return? Why would you think I would do that? Cthulhu is not your parents who allow you to waste away your life in their basement.

If you want to achieve greatness, you must do it on your own. Turn off your video game console and your computer. Look at the world around you. What would you like to accomplish with your sad, pathetic life?

Once you decide on that, then look at how you will achieve it– school, training, hard work, or combination of all these and more. Greatness is not something achieved overnight – except for a few of course. You need to work and strive. You will hit bumps in the road and make mistakes, but if you learn from them and keep striving you can achieve greatness or at least mediocrity, which compared to what you are now is several steps up.

On the off chance that you do actually manage to achieve something great and wonderful, I success suggest you take lots of pictures and videos of your current pathetic existence so you can use them as marketing materials when you do finally discover a way to motivate others to give you money.

Or you can send $10,000 in unmarked bills to Dear Cthulhu, and he will send you his 12-page pamphlet *Achieving Greatness – How To Do It*. Include another $25 for shipping and handling.

Dear Cthulhu,

I come from a family of hunters. All the men in my family going back generations go out every year and shoot a bunch of animals so we don't spend money buying our meat at the supermarket. Even my great grandpa spent money turning a four-wheeler into a wheelchair so he can go out into the woods to hunt.

I went out once with my dad and my older brother when I was 11. The only thing I managed to shoot was a tree. They teased me about that for years and never let me live it down but I wasn't as much a man as they were.

This year I'm eighteen. I'm going to graduate high school and go to college as far away from my family as I can manage.

Normally when my brother torments me about the time I went hunting he does it just in front of family. The thing is now he's got this super-hot girlfriend and ever since the first time I saw her, I can't stop thinking about her. To add to my misery, Hottie is some sort of hunter groupie. The idea of her man killing animals gets her hot.

For years all the men in my family have been hunting this one buck who has a birthmark of a white dot in a circle in the middle of his forehead that looks like a bulls-eye. Apparently, at one point or another, they've all seen him, all tried to bag him, but Bullseye is smarter than all of them and has evaded them.

My brother was bragging to Hottie about how he was finally going to take down Bullseye this year and she started squeezing the parts of her body that have occupied my dreams. Then I said maybe I'd go out hunting this year and I'd be the one to bag Bullseye.

That's when my brother started relating the story of the tree I shot. I countered that we used the hole to put in a spout to make maple syrup with, so it's not like I didn't contribute food. I also pointed out that the best they ever got was a ten pointer but I got a thousand and six-pointer.

Hottie laughed. My brother, on the other hand, said there was no way I'd be able to bag a squirrel, let alone Bullseye.

Hottie then laughed at me and testosterone took over my mouth. I said not only would I bag Bullseye but I'd hit him right in its birthmark.

Hottie commented on how hot that would be and my brother pointed out how impossible it would be. I, in turn, asked him what he would give me if I did it. He said he'd let me sleep with Hottie. Then Hottie said she would sleep with me no matter what he said if I managed to bag Bullseye. And if I managed to shot him through his bulls-eye birthmark she'll take me to her cabin in the woods for the weekend and make sure I couldn't walk home under my own power.

So for the first time since I was eleven, I went out and got myself a hunting license. For every day of deer season, I went out into the woods in bright orange gear in search of this white whale of a deer. I didn't see Bullseye but did take some shots at what I thought were deer. I hit three trees, a boulder, and a lot of dirt but nothing that was alive.

By the end of the first week, I was tired and sore. I was willing to take any buck I could get, get some white paint and paint the bulls-eye on and hope for the best. I tried but I couldn't even find a deer. At one point I was so desperate I considered shooting a cow but realized that wouldn't fool anybody.

On the last day of deer season, I had all but given up and was driving home when there in front of me on the road was Bullseye! I slammed my foot on the brake and the screeching of my tires made Bullseye run to the other side of the road where he got clipped by a pickup truck and flew into a ditch. The driver got out of his pickup truck, saw that only his fender was bent a little bit and took off.

I pulled over and went to the ditch. It was definitely Bullseye and he was still twitching. I got my rifle, aimed at his birthmark and pulled the trigger. Maybe it was luck, maybe it was fate, but the bullet went right in the center of the birthmark.

I tied Bullseye up on the hood of my car and drove home. As luck would have it, not only was my great-grandfather, grandfather, father, and brother there but so were some assorted uncles and cousins. Not to mention Hottie.

I pulled into the driveway and honked my horn. The men all turned and saw the bulls-eye birthmark. I never seen so many men's jaws drop. My brother even dropped his beer.

The whole family came over to examine the elusive buck. My grandfather spit on his fingers and tried to wipe birthmark off, so I guess it was good I didn't try the paint trick. Apparently one of my uncles had already tried that years ago and it didn't work.

Hottie took my hand, lead me into the garage and followed through on her promise.

That weekend we went to the cabin and it was amazing. My father butchered the deer but brought the head to a taxidermist he knew and now it's mounted on the wall above my bed. Now every time Hottie comes over to the house, I ask her to come with me into my room and she sees the head and I'm the one who gets mounted.

It's really pissing my brother off and he even told my dad on me. I countered by telling my dad the deal he made. Bro had said that I could sleep with his girlfriend and but he never mentioned anything about me having to stop sleeping with her.

Dad agreed with me and it's been great, even if Bro does bring Hottie around the house a lot less these days. He won't break up with her because the odds of him getting another girl that good looking are next to impossible. So now I visit Hottie over at her apartment. I bring a selfie of me in front of the deer head that I had blown up to poster size and printed out on a canvas frame. It works almost as good as the real thing.

The teasing has stopped and my family finally thinks I become a man. The problem is, the entire family is already talking about next hunting season and how they all want to go out with me so I could teach them my secrets. I have no hunting secrets. If a deer has been hit by a car and is twitching helplessly in front of me, I can shoot it. Otherwise, I've got zilch.

If I go out with everyone, they'll find out I'm a phony. And the worst of it is if Hottie finds out, she'll stop sleeping with me. What am I going to do?

– Hoax Hunter in Hawkshaw

Dear Hawkshaw,

Do not feel bad about not being a hunter. There is no shame in it. Hunters must have their prey. Although Cthulhu enjoys a good hunt, Cthulhu finds it all too easy, even when he gives the humans a head start.

However, you have managed to turn a happy accident into a life-changing experience and should be commended for it. You're also intelligent enough to realize that it cannot last forever.

You have two options. One is to go outside of your area and hire expert hunters to teach you marksmanship and the ability to track then practice until next hunting season so you will actually be able to impress your relations, although as Cthulhu understands it, much of hunting for many hunters is an excuse to get away from their families and drink beer in the woods. If that is the case with your family, bring lots of alcohol and they will be easier to impress.

The other simpler option is to go away to college as you planned and every year during hunting season make sure you have a project or test that you must study for which will make you unable to come home to hunt. You can continue this practice through your adulthood as long as you relocate far away from your family. If you want to continue to one-up them, you can make friends in your area with local hunters and offer them money to allow you to pose with the animals they kill and send the pictures home to your family.

True, this will cut down on the amount you're able to procreate with your brother's girlfriend, but let us be honest. There's a limited future with that anyway. Someone else will come along and actually take her hunting with them. When she actually sees someone shoot and kill an animal, it will trump your trophy and she will drop you and go for them instead. This way if you come home at non-hunting season times, you may be able to string out the procreation for at least a few years, although if your brother ends up marrying her your relationship could end up causing some bumps in the marriage.

You might be better suited to finding a procreational partner who actually finds you attractive and optimally even cares for you. With humans, that won't last forever, but it is a better basis than what you have now because I just received a letter from your brother and my advice to him will definitely put a crimp in your procreation.

Dear Cthulhu,

I've been having issues with my girlfriend and my little brother the wimp. I asked her to the prom and she turned me down flat. Later that night, I saw her outside her house watching a bunch of rabbits. I was kind of pissed off at the rejection so I shot one of the bunnies with a BB gun. I assumed she'd be mad and we'd be even. Instead, it got her hot and she came over, ripped my clothes off right in the field and made me a man. And she went to prom with me and we've been together ever since. Hunting turns her on and I'm a good hunter.

Problem is I've been telling her for years about Bullseye, this deer my entire family has been hunting for decades. He's a wiley sort and none of us have ever been able to shoot him. I told her about how I was going to get Bullseye and every time I did, it led to a good night, if you know what I mean.

The problem is my brother overheard me once and claimed he was going to do it. I laughed and made the mistake of saying if he managed to do it that he could sleep with my girlfriend. To my surprise, she agreed. Then to my utter shock, the wimp actually managed to do it. I have no idea how but ever since the wimp managed to nail the deer he's been he's nailing my girlfriend.

The wimp is afraid of guns and a horrible shot. Now my little brother is making my life a living hell. This wimp could never hunt like the rest of the family. We are men who bring home meat. The only thing he ever shot before this year was a tree.

My dad had the head stuffed and the wimp hung it in his bedroom. Every time my girl sees it up close, she gets naked and jumps on top of the wimp. It's putting a cramp in our relationship. I even complained to my dad but apparently because I didn't bother to say he could sleep with her just once that my permission is implied.

Normally, I'd dump a girl who did this to me, but this girl is better looking than movie stars and the things she'll do you in bed will make your legs melt.

Wimp even took a picture of himself in front of the deer head and goes over to her house. He shows that and she jumps on him there too.

What can I do to stop him from doing it with my girl?

– Cuckold Hawkshaw Hunter

Dear Cuckold,

I assumed you tried asking both of them to stop. If this failed, it would appear that your girlfriend is more interested in procreating with whoever has bagged the biggest buck than in being faithful.

You really don't have much of a future with this woman. Should you decide to marry her, she will likely cheat on you with whatever hunter brings back the biggest deer. Or worse, you may meet someone who hunts big game and when she sees those heads mounted on the wall, you will be history.

However, there is a simple solution you're missing to taking care of your brother procreating with your girlfriend. You point out that the mounted head is what turns her on to procreate with him. Simply wait until he is not around, take the deer head off his wall and get rid of it. Then find his picture of it and destroy that as well. You might have to go into his phone or computer to erase the original so does not make another copy. If you do that, then take your girlfriend out to the woods and have her watch you kill something. It should decrease her interest in your sibling and increase it for you, at least until someone else kills something bigger and better.

Dear Cthulhu,

I've read with interest the letters from the one-time Broadway actor and his problems. Well, let me tell you, I wish I had his problems. I love to sing, but the problem is no one else seems to love it or even like it. I can't even find anyone who'll even tolerate it or sit still long enough for me to finish a song. I've been trying to take singing lessons for years, but no instructor has ever made it past the second class. Most quit minutes into the first.

I've included an MP3 of my singing. I want you to tell me if you think I have the potential to make it as a singer.

– Crooner from Coco Beach

Dear Crooner,

I listened to the song that you sent to Cthulhu. At first, I thought I had gotten the wrong file. The one I received sounded like sounded like a cat with a chainsaw fighting off a horde of locusts in a blender filled with broken glass. It was horrendous. A human being exposed to these noises for any length of time would be driven completely and utterly mad quicker than reading any section of the Necronomicon.

Cthulhu loved it!

Cthulhu does not think you have what it takes to make it is as a traditional human singer. However, Cthulhu would like to hire you to sing at a gathering of members of my cult that have irked me, as well as several other annoying humans. I will pay you to perform including the rebroadcast rights. There are a few elder ones who have displeased me over the eons and I think sending them a copy of your concert would be an excellent way to show my displeasure and extract revenge of the same time.

I don't think you'll be a star but perhaps we can use your voice to help certain stars and planets align in order to bring forth a new age of darkness upon this world.

That or consider joining a death metal band as the lead singer.

Dear Cthulhu,

As far as I'm concerned, I'm one of the most accomplished women – no, people – in the entire history of the world. Why just in the last month I have cured someone of cancer, won the Boston Marathon, spent time on the international space station, won Nobel Prizes for peace and for my chocolate soufflé. And modesty forbids me from going into detail about my threesome with Tom Cruise and Hugh Jackman, but it was hot!

The problem is most people don't take my accomplishments seriously and I'm not sure if it's because I'm a woman or because I did it all in my dreams. That's right, I'm the ultimate dream warrior. Yet despite everything I've managed to do, when I offer people the benefit of my wisdom and experience, they often make fun of me and ignore what I'm telling them to do.

When I told my one friend they could get rid of her cancer by using stem cells and a hot glue gun, she looked at me as if I was mad. But she did ask her doctor. That quack said no one had ever heard of such a thing.

When I called Harvard to have them send me a copy of my diploma, they said they had no record of it and hung up on me when I explained how I dreamed I had graduated from there with high honors with a dual major in brain surgery and puppetry.

Then the other night when I was out at a five-star restaurant, I snuck back into the kitchen to give the chef a couple of pointers, telling him that butterscotch and curry were the keys to making the best duck *l'orange* that he'd ever taste. You'd think someone in his position would be thrilled to get advice from someone like me, but no. He had security throw me out and wouldn't even give me my food in a doggie bag.

So my dear Cthulhu, as one of the few on this planet who is accomplished as I am, how do I get people to take my experiences seriously? (Oh and I have some included some pointers for you as an attachment on how to terrorize and take over the planet. You're going to love it.)

– Beautiful Dreamer in Buffalo

Dear Buffalo,

There is a reason why people do not take your claims of skill and experience seriously – they are utter nonsense. In human, dreams are your minds way of processing the day's events and dealing with stress. The events of life influence your dreams, not the other way around, unlike Cthulhu whose dreams can influence the entire world and universe. In fact. right now Cthulhu might lie dreaming and when I awake you will find that you have been nothing but a figment of that dream and I will either make you cease to be or live in horror and terror, depending on my mood that day.

Dear Cthulhu,

I'm a farmer. My father was a farmer, my grandfather was a farmer, my great-grandfather was a farmer. You get the idea. We have been farming a long time and it's not get any easier. I have a small family farm and it's getting harder and harder to compete with the big corporate farm collectives. Seems like each year I'm working harder and making less money. Plus having to figure out ways to use more land, some of which hasn't been farmed in generations.

I was plowing some new ground on my Massey Ferguson I noticed a flurry of money trailing behind me. I've got off my tractor and I went back and found twenty, fifty, and hundred dollar bills all over my field. Not being a fool, I picked them all up. I just couldn't figure out where they'd come from where they came from.

I know there ain't no such thing as a money tree, so I went back through the dirt I'd plowed and saw a bag sticking up through the dirt. I dug around it and it was full of money. I kept digging and found five more bags. They were older bills from before when they started changing all the money around. Then it dawned on me where they come from. 'Bout thirty-five years ago when I was nine, the bank in the next town over was robbed of half a million dollars and the robbers were later killed in a shootout with police and the money was never found.

I counted up the cash and added up to just about five hundred thousand dollars, so this is probably the haul from that bank job. That bank closed up years ago after some bad investments in polecat futures, so I couldn't exactly give them the money back.

Should I keep the money? Would it be legal and moral? I really could use the cash, because my wife left me for her female goat yoga instructor a ways back. Our divorce is final so she wouldn't get any of this, but if it's not supposed to be mine I guess it's best if I turn it in. I'm very conflicted. What should I do?

    – Farmer with a Windfall in Winett

Dear Windfall,

As Cthulhu as has often pointed out, I am not an attorney as there are some seas too dark even for me to swim in. However, I am quite an authority on morality.

The federal statute of limitations on the bank robbery was up five years after it occurred. The bank likely got their money back from their insurance company, so if you could find out who bought the bank's assets and gave the money back to them, they would only have to turn it over to the insurance company so you giving it to the bank doesn't benefit them at all.

As you identify yourself as a moral man, you likely have several personality flaws including that you will feel guilty if you perceive that you've done something wrong. If you think that might be the case, you can always turn in the money and the insurance company would claim it and might give you a reward or finder's fee equal to a small percentage of the full amount. That way you get to rest easier at night and still get a little cash in your pocket.

One other thing to consider – just because you found the money in the field doesn't mean you could get away with just spending it with no consequences. Very often banks have numbered bills which can be identified and he could still show up on a registry even twenty-five years later. An overzealous lawman might try and implicate you in the robbery, despite the fact that you are only nine years old at the time.

Cthulhu would advise consulting an actual attorney to see if there's a way that you can claim having found the money and still get to keep it. Or you can launder it through my cult for a fifty-five percent cut.

Dear Cthulhu,

I am in the first stages of transitioning from man to woman. While I am working on it with both surgery and movement classes, I am not yet the most attractive woman but I want to be but I still have many masculine qualities.

The problem is my state has recently passed some oppressive laws regarding going to the bathroom and where I can do it. I was wondering where you weighed in on the bathroom debate.

– Pigeon Holed in Pigeon River

Dear Pigeon,

There are many times Cthulhu simply does not understand how some aspects of humanity treat other aspects. This bathroom debacle is one of those times. For one thing, from Cthulhu's viewpoint, you all look alike regardless of race or gender. I have to work very hard to tell you apart. You should be united together to fight off the forces around you that want you destroyed, but instead, you work at destroying each other from within, not realizing you are all generally the same.

Cthulhu does not think people who feel they were born the wrong gender and have made an effort to change should be singled out for negative treatment or made to feel like they should bring a bucket wherever they go to put their excrement into. If you are in a place you feel you may have a problem, consider a bathroom buddy, someone who cares and is obviously the same gender you identify with to go with you into the bathroom. It is my understanding that the female of the species has a herd mentality when it comes to putting their excretions and excrement into the small flushing devices, so going together will not raise any eyebrows. If you are alone and there is a family bathroom available and there is worry of your safety, use that.

There are several products for sale which allow you to put a body camera on you that will record what you do throughout the day and they have become relatively inexpensive. If someone does give you trouble, particularly the owner of a business, you can record them and place it on the Internet. You will likely garner enough sympathy for like-minded individuals to protest the business owner's poor judgment. It is possible that it may hurt his business or even close it for a time. As this happens to more owners, they may decide it is not worth the trouble to bother people when they are excreting and situations such as these might decrease. Just turn the camera off when in the actual bathroom.

Dear Cthulhu,

I recently started dating this wonderful girl that I met on a school trip. We're both in tenth grade. Unfortunately, my mother just got a promotion and we have to move a half hour away. We both discussed and we're more than willing to give the long-distance relationship thing a try and try to meet up on the weekends. There's a problem – her family is old-fashioned and act like the Amish. They don't have the Internet and they won't let her have a cell phone until she can figure out a way to pay for it for herself.

How are we going to keep in touch?
– Starcrossed Lovers in Schenectady

Dear Schenectady,

This may come as a shock to you, but people were able were able to communicate with each other before the invention of the Internet or cell phones and texting. I suspect her parents have a landline. That is a telephone that uses wires to give and receive messages and you would likely be able to call her on that. Also, people use these things called letters, similar to the email you sent Cthulhu except they write them out by hand on paper, put them in an envelope on which they then write the person's address, place a stamp on it and put it in a mailbox. Then through the magic of the post office, the letter will be taken to the person they addressed it to. That person will open it, read the letter and if they are so inclined will write back repeating the process. While it does not have the instant gratification of texting or emailing, it might make you appreciate the messages more. Plus, you can add personalized touches like drawings and scented perfumes and colognes which can not yet be done electronically.

Dear Cthulhu,

I've got a huge problem, and by huge I mean *huge*. In fact, maybe you could say I have two huge problems.

My coworker – let's call her Boobzilla – has tremendous hooters. Seriously. This babe could clean up on a stripper pole, but no, for some reason she didn't go into the profession that makes the most sense for the way she looks. Instead, she chose to work in an office and that's not fair to me. I can barely get any work done because I am too busy staring at her massive ta-tas. For the most part, Boobzilla does dress conservatively and wears loose clothing, but let's be honest – her chest is so massive even loose clothing is tight, if you know what I mean. But every so often she'll wear a plunging neckline with a push-up bra and my work output is shot for the day.

When she dresses like that, with everything hanging out I just want, no I need to touch her boobies. Unfortunately, if I did that I'd be charged with some sort of stupid assault. It's not fair. She's going to have them hanging out there and make me stare at them all day long, the least she could do was give me an occasional feel, right? Hell, I'd be willing to slip some singles in there to make it worthwhile, maybe even throw in a twenty for a lap dance during lunch.

How do you think I should broach the subject?

– Boobzilla Watcher in Boise

Dear Boise,

You seem to have several misconceptions about how the world and social interaction works. Just because a woman has a shapely figure and chooses to show a little bit of skin, that does not make her a sex object or stripper whose purpose in life it is to amuse you.

Just because your coworker has well-endowed mammalian protuberances, that does not mean they are there to be your play toys. And just because she has them "hanging out" does not give you the right to touch them. Cthulhu goes around all the time with my tentacles "hanging out". Do you think that I do not notice all the staring? Most humans have the good sense to know that they are *my* tentacles and I share them with who I want to. If you were to try and touch my tentacles without my permission, you'd be missing that hand awful quick. This woman may not take kindly and she may lay you out or have you arrested.

And just because she looks one way does not give you the right to assign her what kind of profession she can have. Whether she wants to be a dancer or a nuclear physicist it is none of your business.

This is not to say that touching her mammalian protuberances is entirely out of the question, but you would have to earn that right. Have you ever considered talking to your coworker like she was a fellow human being? Make her laugh, do nice things for her. Maybe ask her out for a cup of coffee or even on a date. If she says no, that means *no*.

However, if she says yes, try to romance her, woo her. Get to know the real person behind the mammalian protuberances. Since like Cthulhu, she is likely constantly inundated with unwanted stares, the effort might actually be appreciated. And for Lovecraft's sake, look at her eyes. I hate it when people just blatantly stare at my tentacles.

And if you become romantically involved, you may indeed get to touch that which you desire, although Cthulhu advises not doing it at the workplace.

Dear Cthulhu,

I am very disappointed in my choice of presidential candidates this year. Occasionally I will see a meme on the Internet suggesting that you might be running for president. Is it true?

– Curious Voter in Vermont

Dear Voter,

Cthulhu has addressed this before. Cthulhu has no desire to run for political office. While I can appreciate the sentiment of wanting great Cthulhu to rule over you, when it happens it will not be by election but by but how it should be – by alignment of stars in a show of deadly and primal force.

Besides, it's much more fun to pull the strings of those who think they're in charge from behind the scenes.

Dear Cthulhu,

I have an addiction that I'm not proud of. I'm addicted to strip clubs and it's kind of unusual I guess because I'm a woman. I just love going to see guys dance around and take off their clothes.

My husband has a problem with my hobby and he banned me from going to any clubs and it was making me nuts. My hubby has a great personality and is a good provider, but his body leaves a lot to be desired. He's flabby and not much to look at. You think he'd be happy I went to strip clubs because I always came home horny and he made out like a bandit. Apparently, the idea of me shoving dollar bills down another guy's G string is too much for his fragile ego to take.

After three months I was going crazy. I needed to see some fine naked man flesh bad. It's gotten to the point where I was debating about becoming a peeping Thomasina at a frat house that's about a mile from our home.

Instead, fortune smiled on me and our dishwasher broke. My salvation came in the form of "Dale", the handyman my husband hired to fix the dishwasher. Dale was so hot, with bulging muscles that were straining against the fabric of his thin T-shirt, that I had to see more. I offered him some lemonade and then "accidentally" spilled the lemonade on his shirt. I told him I felt horrible and took the shirt from him and offered to wash it. Like a good boy, he took off the shirt and gave it to me. I put it in the washer on the 60 minute cycle. Dale fixed the dishwasher in twenty minutes but by the time his t-shirt came out of the dryer, I had him shirtless and talking to me for an hour on top of that. Even better, when I gave him back to the shirt it shrunk and showed off even more of his beautiful pecs and abs.

Man, I nailed my husband hard that night. I was good for about a week before my addiction started kicking in again so I accidentally broke a burner on the stove. Like a good little husband, my spouse called Dale again. This time I had cheese fondue waiting and offered him some. And yes, I accidentally dropped some on his shirt. The burner was fixed in ten, but he was there for an hour and a half.

Now I'm breaking stuff at least once, sometimes twice a week depending on how needy I am. My husband thinks our house has become a money pit and wants to sell it and move. I don't have the heart to tell him what I'm doing and unfortunately, the repairs are costing more than the strip clubs did and money's tight.

While it's nice to have my own personal stripper for an hour and a half and it's fun to watch him fix stuff. he refuses to dance and I've tried playing all sorts of music for him.

I really love my house and don't want to have to move. Should I sneak around during lunch and go to a strip club on the sly or keep breaking stuff so Dale comes to fix stuff and me.

Before you answer, I feel I should point out that while I may look and touch just a little, I've never done anything beyond that. I've never cheated on my husband nor do I plan to. What should I do?

– G-string Addiction in Galveston

Dear Galveston,

It sounds like while you are being deceitful while not actually breaking any of your vows. However, in Cthulhu's experience sneaking around to do something that one's spouse has expressly asked one not to can have very negative consequences.

Perhaps you could discuss this addiction with your husband. There are clubs that have sections for men and women to observe people of both genders taking their clothes off. Many couples will go to the separate sections and then hook up again later, basically because they are not attractive enough to get someone that they find attractive so they use the strippers as a substitute. This sounds like what you are doing. Perhaps if he went and saw some naked human females, he would not feel as threatened by it.

Another option would be for you to encourage him to hit the gym that perhaps he can sculpt himself into the type of body that would float your boat as people say. You can do the same for him. I'm sure you would be able to convince him to dance as well as long as you returned the favor.

If the gym is taking too long, perhaps you could seek out someone who sells steroids that would increase his muscle bulk. There are some dangerous side effects which you should be careful to monitor, but at least that way you might have a happier marriage

Dear Cthulhu,

My parents had always told me I wouldn't amount to much, which makes a certain amount of sense because they never did and I came from them. They had me convinced I'd never get to go to college so I dropped out of high school at sixteen and I started working for a local diner. I worked my way up from busboy to fry cook.

Business for the diner had kind of dropped down a little bit as we became surrounded by all these weird food joints that sell healthier and other types of food.

One day my boss made a mistake and ordered too many veggies and was going to throw them out so I threw a bunch in the fryer and the boss gave them out as freebies to some of his regulars. Turns out people loved them and he started advertising that they were organic and vegan, but I'm pretty sure he didn't know what either of those things meant. I'm pretty sure that he thinks organic means that they were the once living things. I have no idea if they qualified as vegan or not.

There's this one customer who was really hot that I had dated. She was an actual vegan but after a month she cheated on me with a sous chef.

I was pretty upset so the next time she came in she wanted some of our fried veggies I poured a bunch of bacon grease into the fryer. Turns out everyone loves bacon, even vegans. She told her vegan friends about them and suddenly we are the new hotspot with people coming in for my fried vegetables.

My boss asked me what I did differently, but I knew if I told him he'd have me stop adding it. Plus, he's been threatening to fire me on and off for the last few months so I told him it was an old secret family recipe.

Business at the diner's booming so much that an organic startup company that's been doing pretty well for itself has approached me on the sly asking me for my secret recipe. They offered me ten grand upfront and two percent of the net sales for the frozen version of my recipe.

I could really use the money but I doubt I will be to convince these guys that bacon is vegan.

Do you think I'd be able to convince them to let me work in secret in the factory as a paying job and get the extra money on the side?

– Fry Cook in Frisco

Dear Cook,

It is highly doubtful that any food company is going to let you work in secret in their factory. They are governed by a Board of Health and all sorts of laws which include them having to list all the ingredients they use in a product on the packaging so unless you can find a vegetarian bacon substitute, you'll have to stick with working at the diner.

Also, for future reference the percentage of the net is worthless. Always get a percentage of the gross.

Dear Cthulhu,

It's me again – the former Broadway actor who hijacked a show and who is now blackballed from the stage.

After the mix-up when I showed up at the memorial service for the poor person who died from anesthesia during a gender reassignment surgery, I was beaten badly and charged with a hate crime.

You'll be happy to know that the hate crime charges were dropped. I made my arguments in person to them that it just wasn't true. They just didn't believe me, so to prove my sincerity I donned women's clothing, got up on stage, and sang a medley of show tunes from my past performances.

Turns out they loved me. In fact, I've now found work in a cabaret of female impersonators. It's not Broadway and it's only two times a week, but the crowds are enthusiastic and it pays the bills.

In fact, those who once beat me until I was unconscious now feel bad about it and have even thrown a fundraiser to help cover my medical expenses.

I get to sing what I want and I do my own choreography. I'm in heaven. For the first time in years. I'm truly happy and found a place where I belong. Broadway was nice but now I have a home.

The only fly in the ointment is that I don't make a very good-looking woman. Some of the other performers have suggested I get surgery, either to make my face more feminine while others have suggested getting breast implants all the way up to having a sex change.

I've never been either heterosexual, homosexual, or even bisexual. Truth be told, I've never found anyone more desirable than myself so I guess I'm self-sexual. However, my self-image is that of a man. I have no problem acting or dressing as a woman, but I don't really want to become a woman. However, I'm loathe to lose what I've found. What should I do?

– Gave My Regards to Broadway and Finally Did It My Way

Dear Regards,

Cthulhu is a staunch supporter of anyone, even humans, being true to their own selves. Unless, of course, there's a good reason to do otherwise. The community that you have found yourself a home in is noted for being understanding and tolerant of others as they have experienced the polar opposite in their lives. I do not think your ability to perform will suffer if you do not have these augmentation surgeries. Instead of going under the knife, work toward maximizing the assets you do have. Talk to the other performers and get makeup tips.

Remembering that most humans look-alike to Cthulhu, but even I have been impressed by the makeup artistry of some of these performers. Work on improving your wardrobe to fit your body type. Consider wearing a girdle, elastic shapewear, or even a corset. You can buy fluid sacks that mimic the female breast and can be worn under a bra while performing. Invest in a quality wig.

And since you fancy yourself to be such an actor, spend more time studying your fellow performers and the female of the species so you may imitate them better. All these will improve your craft without resorting to having to do something to your body that you prefer not to.

Dear Cthulhu,

I'm a farmer in Colorado where after a long and protracted fight, marijuana has finally been legalized. It's been a boon to the whole state. Everyone's making money hand over fist from the government to the growers to the hotels and restaurants because of the booming tourist industry. As a farmer who barely gets by some years, I'd like to get in on this and start growing so I can get rich too.

The problem is my wife. She was one of the most staunch and vocal opponents of the legalization. She tells anyone who will listen that marijuana is the Devil's handiwork. She lobbied long and hard to keep it from happening and she's been impossible to live with ever since she lost.

Her whole issue with marijuana stems back to when she was a teenager. It seems she tried a joint once and she claims it ruined her life. She exaggerates a bit. To hear her tell it, after smoking one joint, she ran naked through the biggest social event of the year and ended up homeless. I was there and what really happened is she smoked a joint at a high school prom, danced like a maniac, and ate every snack there. Then for some reason, she thought it would be a really good idea to take off her prom dress and streak through the dance. But she wasn't naked – she had on a slip. She kept running and fell asleep in the doorway of the local hardware store and woke up to next to Bob the town hobo. (We still called them that back then.)

She was voted class streaker in the yearbook and most likely to be to do drugs and never really got over it. To be honest, it loosened her up a lot, which is part of why I married her. But that has been steadily worn away by the trials and tribulations of everyday life and now she's more uptight than she ever was.

I'm afraid if I tell her what I want to do, she'll divorce me. To be honest, I wouldn't miss her so much, but she'd probably take half of my family farm, which means I'd make half the money.

I was thinking that maybe I would try and slip her some

marijuana-laced cookies or something. They're all over the place now and see if it loosens her up any.

What do you think?

– Life Not Going Up in Smoke in Colorado

Dear Smoke,

As tempting as it might be to slip your wife a drug, Cthulhu must recommend against it. If she has an extreme reaction as she did in the past when she comes down shown she will know what you did and not only could she divorce you, but she could press criminal charges against you.

You could go out to one of your local restaurants that serve these products and ask for a sample plate or some such and see if she tries any of it. Or you could see if you get invited to any local parties where it is served in the *hors-d'oeuvres* and desserts and simply not mention it to your wife.

You could try logic, explaining to her how your lives would be better off making more money. In fact, you could tell her that you would donate five percent of the profits into a fund for her to continue her fight against legalization. I'm sure there are others who feel similarly to how she does and she might see some justice in using the profits from selling marijuana to try to make it illegal again.

Dear Cthulhu,

Ever since I was a kid all I ever dreamed about was being an astronaut. I had posters on my bedroom walls of the Apollo rockets and space shuttles. Now we don't even have a space program so how the heck am I going to become an astronaut? That and I might've failed the physical to get into NASA eleven times on account of skipping exercise to sit in front of my computer and eat potato chips with melted cheese and chili all day.

Like many of your other readers, I too feel I've been betrayed by the American dream. They told me I could be anything I wanted and later told me that becoming what I wanted would involve ridiculous amounts of hard work and dedication. Why can't NASA just realize that this is what I want and make me an astronaut now? Just wave the physical requirements. They've done it before for scientists. That's discrimination just because I'm not a scientist. What difference should it make to them whether or not I have or haven't dedicated years of my life to getting a degree that would be some use to the world and space exploration?

Is there some way I can force NASA to make me an astronaut? I was thinking that maybe I'd go for a tour at Cape Canaveral and then "accidentally" trip and "hurt myself". Then I would see them for like a billion dollars and agree to forgo the money if they send me up on a Russian rocket to spend a week at the international space station. I'd love to spend more time, but I only get two weeks' vacation a year and they won't let me take them at the same time. Unless maybe NASA could have one of their astronauts work the fryer at Burger Bucket for me. Meanwhile, I could fry up some good snacks for the crew of the space station. They only seem to eat out of those little bags so I'm sure they'll appreciate some fires or deep-fried cupcakes.

Do you think it's a good plan? Or do you have a better one?

– Spaced Out in San Dimas

Dear Spaced,

Cthulhu would like to point out that humans do not have an innate right to have other people make them become something just because they want it. Do you think Cthulhu would have gotten Earth if he hadn't fought hundreds of other older ones for the right? Not that I don't regret my choice every other day, especially when I open up my e-mail.

No one is going to give me dominion over the Earth. When the time comes, I'm going to have to take it. If you want to be an astronaut train, pass the physical, and learn other skills that they will need. Study and get a doctorate. That or figure a way to make a great deal of money because the Russians are allowing private citizens to go up in their rockets. Prices start at twenty million. Save up that much money and you can be an astronaut.

Or the least expensive means of space travel available to humans is via a high altitude balloon to nineteen miles above the Earth for a mere seventy-five thousand dollars, something an average human could actually save with some hard work.

As for your plan, it has too many faults for me to even begin to list. NASA facilities are very important to your government. As such they have surveillance which will pick up you pretending to hurt yourself. Unless you have a convincing MRI or lose a limb, not only will you not have a case, you might be arrested for trying to extort the federal government. Not to mention if you are hurt, you are disqualified to go up in space. If you tell them you're not hurt then you no longer have a lawsuit so it would not work.

Another flaw is the idea of frying foods in space. Without gravity, the boiling oil would float out and possibly hurt the astronauts – and make a huge mess – which is why it is not done and they specially package their food.

In the long run, you likely will not do anything different with your existence than you are doing now. Just be thankful in terms of your skill set and employment that your employer always ends taking people's orders with the phrase "Do you want fries with that?"

Dear Cthulhu,

I've been married for 23 years. I'd say happily married, but I don't like to overtly lie. It is not that my wife is a horrible person, at least to anybody else but me. My four kids are wonderful, at least in public and around other people. When we're at home, it's a whole other story. They fight and are exceedingly cruel to each other. All my wife seems to do is yell at them and at me but I give her credit. She works as a rodeo clown and does the lion's share of work around the house.

Not that I'm perfect. I yell and lose my cool at times too. It's just this is not what I pictured my life to be like. When I married my wife, she was my best friend. I thought it would always stay that way. Instead, we're practically strangers, roommates raising children together. Not that I'm looking to leave. I made vows and I take those seriously.

The problem is we live in a small three-bedroom house with only one bathroom. The only time I get to be alone and have relative peace and quiet is my thirty-minute commute to and from work. The rest of my life is taking kids to afterschool activities and sports. Between the four of them, I don't get a spare moment to sit and relax until the kids go to bed. Then I tend to sit in front of the TV for a little bit before going to bed. I try and spend time with my wife, but she'd rather read a romance novel than actually try to have some romance with her husband.

The top it all off I'm getting older, fluffier, and grayer. It wasn't supposed to be like this.

A few months ago, my Uncle Irving passed away. We'd been close when I was a kid and he was very generous to me as well. He left me his thirty-foot-long RV. This thing is old but built solid. We have just enough room to fit it on the side of our house.

To be honest, the thing's been a godsend. I don't have my own space in the house, but now I can go out and hide in the RV. It's got a refrigerator, microwave, couch, and a bed. And it has its own bathroom and shower. I suddenly have my own home outside my home.

Having my own space, away from the fighting in the yelling the bickering has made me a much happier person.

Here's the thing – I get a week more vacation than my wife does so usually I end up taking it and spending it at home with a honey-do list.

My Uncle Irving however always took his extra week vacation to drive out to California to have it serviced at the manufacturer. It's a good two-day drive. I always thought it was weird that he would take a trip by himself with the RV, but he had seven kids. Now that I have four, I understand.

My wife and kids have no interest in taking the RV on vacation anywhere. My wife suggested I sell it but I told her no way. I also told her that I was going to need to take it to California to have it serviced and that I would use my extra week of vacation to do it.

We'd been close with Uncle Irving, so my wife knows about his annual trek and I was surprised when she agreed to it. Problem is I feel a little bit guilty. I mean I'm a husband and a father. I should be with my family. Except my family drives me nuts. I think this week would be a way to help me keep my sanity and actually be a better father and husband. I'm not looking to use the trip as an excuse to cheat or do anything else wrong. So why do I feel guilty? And should I do it or just stay home and paint the fence?

– Mobile Homeowner in Mobile City

Dear Mobile,

It is rare that I actually get a person writing in who was already doing the right thing. You are not breaking any vows, you're being honest about what you are doing. Your home situation honestly sounds like a nightmare, yet you endure and do not break your vows. You toil for no reason other than it's what you are supposed to do. As far as Cthulhu is concerned, you are a perfectly adequate little human and will one day make a wonderful servant when Cthulhu rises.

The simple truth of the matter is guilt is one of the ways society keeps others in line. They drill into your head right and wrong and then make you feel bad when you do wrong. With some people, this can carry over to the extreme and they feel guilty for doing something that others would not even blink at.

Go on your road trip, have your RV serviced, and have a little adventure. Stop off and see the sights, take a selfie yourself in front of the largest ball of twine. Stop at roadside diners and have conversations with people you'll never see again. Have fun and then return to your mind-numbing life with the knowledge at least you have a week next year that you can look forward to.

Have A Dark Day.

PATRICK THOMAS is the award-winning author of almost 40 books including the beloved fantasy humor Murphy's Lore series, which includes *Tales From Bulfinche's Pub, Fools' Day, Through The Drinking Glass, Shadow Of The Wolf, Redemption Road, Bartender Of The Gods, Nightcaps, Empty Graves, The Mug Life* — as well as the future space adventures *Startenders* and *Constellation Prize*.

The Murphy's Lore After Hours spin-offs star the half pixie/ogre Terrorbelle (*Fairy With A Gun, Fairy Rides The Lightning* and *Terrorbelle The Unconquered*); the former demon-possessed serial killer Agent Karver of the Department of Mystic Affairs (*Dead To Rites, Rites of Passage*); the cursed mage Hex (*By Darkness Cursed and By Invocation Only*); Vince Argus, the Soul For Hire (*Greatest Hits*); and Negral, a forgotten Sumerian god who works as Hell's Detective (*Lore & Dysorder* and *Bullets & Brimstone*).

Co-Written with John French and Diane Raetz, his Mystic Investigators paranormal mystery series includes *Mean Streets* and the omnibus edition *Shadows & Bullets & Brimstone* and *Once Upon In Crime. Assassin's Ball*, his first mystery, is also co-written with John French.

His works include the steampunk *As The Gears Turn* and the space epic *Exile & Entrance*. He co-edited *New Blood* and *Hear Them Roar* and was an editor for the magazines *Fantastic Stories of the Imagination* and *Pirate Writings*.

Patrick's darkly humorous advice column Dear Cthulhu has been running since 2005 and includes the collections *Have A Dark Day, Good Advice For Bad People, Cthulhu Knows Best, Cthulhu Happens, Cthulhu Explains It All* and *What Would Cthulhu Do?* Dear Cthulhu appears monthy on the radio show *Destinies: The Voice of Science Fiction* which is hosted by Dr. Howard Margolin.

His short stories have been featured in over sixty anthologies and more than forty-five print magazines.

A number of his books were part of the props department of the CSI television show and Nightcaps was even thrown at a suspect's head. His urban fantasy Fairy With A Gun had been optioned for film and TV by Laurence Fishburne's Cinema Gypsy Productions. Top Men Productions has turned his Soul For Hire Story, *Act of Contrition*, into a short film.

Please drop by www.patthomas.net or follow him at I_PatrickThomas Twitter or www.facebook.com/PatrickThomasAuthor to learn more.

Help is only a Rainbow Away…

"Mix Gaiman's American Gods and Robinson's Callahan's Crosstime Saloon on Prachett's Discworld and you get an idea of Thomas' Murphy's Lore." -David Sherman, author of STARFIST and Demontech

"ENTERTAINING, INVENTIVE AND DELIGHTFULLY CREEPY." -JONATHAN MABERRY, New York Times and Bram Stoker Award Winning Author

"SLICK… ENTERTAINING." -Paul Di Filippo, ASIMOV'S

"HUMOR, OUTRAGEOUS ADVENTURES, & SOME CLEVER PLOT TWISTS." -Don D'Ammassa, SCIENCE FICTION CHRONICLE

PATRICK THOMAS

Shape up...
You only get
ONE Warning

Hell's
Detective

No One Is Above The
Even I

One Last Chance to Save
Happily Ever After

...an a group of heroes including Goldenhair,
...ed Riding Hood and Rapunzel help General
...now White and her dwarven resistance
...ghters defeat the tyrannical Queen Cinderella?
...nd will they succeed before a war with
...onderland destroys everything?

...heir only hope to stop Cinderella's quest
...r power lies with a young girl named
...atience Muffet who carries the fabled
...ards of Cinderella's glass slippers.

...oy Mauritsen's fantasy adventure
...iry tale epic begins with *Shards*
...f The Glass Slipper: Queen Cinder.

**"Fantastic...
A Magnificent Epic!"**
-*Sarah Beth Durst* author of
Into The Wild & Drink, Slay, Love

**"The Brothers Grimm
meets
Lord Of The Rings!"**
-*Patrick Thomas,* author
of the *Murphy's Lore* series

**"Shards is a dark, lush,
full-throttle fantasy
epic that presents
a bold re-imagining
of classic characters."**
-David Wade, creator of
319 Dark Street

**"Roy Mauritsen's
enchanting epic
comes at a time
when fairy tales
are back in the
forefront of
our collective
imagination."**
-Darin Kennedy,
short fiction author

PADWOLF
PUBLISHING

In paperback & e-book
Find out more at:
shardsoftheglassslipper.com
padwolf.com

MYSTIC INVESTIGATORS
BY PATRICK THOMAS
A MYSTIC INVESTIGATORS OMNIBUS
SHADOWS & BRIMSTONE
PATRICK THOMAS & JOHN L. FRENCH
MYSTIC INVESTIGATORS BOOK
MEAN STREETS
PATRICK THOMAS
A MYSTIC INVESTIGATORS OMNIBUS
ONCE UPON IN CRIME
PATRICK THOMAS & DIANE RAETZ
DOWN THESE MEANS STREETS
of Magic & Monsters walk the
MYSTIC INVESTIGATORS